Beverly J James has a passion for writing and for humanity. She believes that love is the single greatest and most powerful force in the universe. God is love.

For my superhero – no one has loved me more or better. You will always be the love of my life. Thank you for changing the direction of my world and giving me life. I love you more than everything. Everything, baby.

Beverly J James

ALSO KNOWN AS...LOVE

AUSTIN MACAULEY PUBLISHERS™
LONDON • CAMBRIDGE • NEW YORK • SHARJAH

Copyright © Beverly J James (2020)

The right of Beverly J James to be identified as author of this work has been asserted by the author in accordance with section 77 and 78 of the Copyright, Designs and Patents Act 1988.

All rights reserved. No part of this publication may be reproduced, stored in a retrieval system, or transmitted in any form or by any means, electronic, mechanical, photocopying, recording, or otherwise, without the prior permission of the publishers.

Any person who commits any unauthorised act in relation to this publication may be liable to criminal prosecution and civil claims for damages.

This is a work of fiction. Names, characters, businesses, places, events, locales, and incidents are either the products of the author's imagination or used in a fictitious manner. Any resemblance to actual persons, living or dead, or actual events is purely coincidental.

A CIP catalogue record for this title is available from the British Library.

ISBN 9781528989985 (Paperback)
ISBN 9781528989992 (ePub e-book)

www.austinmacauley.com

First Published (2020)
Austin Macauley Publishers Ltd
25 Canada Square
Canary Wharf
London
E14 5LQ

Thanks, Melissa for the clarity. Angela and Tiffany, thanks for the faith that helped me go ahead. Sherri, thanks for more than I can say. Jason, my son, my rock – I love you and Tasha. Jayla and Jaxon – you guys are my heart and soul. Thank you, Lord Jesus for forgiving me every day in my weakness and failures and still finding me worthy.

Chapter 1

I should have known that I was going to have problems with this love thing from the beginning of my so-called love life. Way back when I was so in love at 15 that I thought I was ready for sex. Boy was I wrong. I should have known then! But no! I thought I was in love. I truly didn't get it. In my defence, everybody was lying back then saying how great sex was. I know *he* did!

"I promise," he said. "It's going to be so good," he said. I don't know why I believed him, all I know is that my first experience was so painful that I pushed Leslie—(yes, I lost my virginity to a guy named Leslie—okay?) anyway, I pushed him off me and punched him as hard as I could! What had started out as a lovemaking session turned into a big fight, and we never spoke to each other again.

So, the stage was set. Though my first sexual experience hurt tremendously, I did not give up. And the truth is, some form of love has been hurting me ever since. Yet, I stayed the course.

Finally, after years of trying and losing, and trying and losing, I met Harry. Harry said he wanted to marry me on our second date. I liked that. And though I had seen many warning signs along the way, we married after two and a half months of knowing (or not knowing) each other. He disappeared on our wedding day for nearly four hours and actually confessed that he had been with his ex. We were married for a total of 18 months that consisted of numerous affairs by him, me perfecting the art of being a sleuth, several bouts of bloodshed and destruction of property and him finally admitting that he did not want to be married to me anymore. Unfortunately, even with all of that, I thought I still wanted to be with him.

The divorce was devastating for me—but I made the Dean's List in the middle of it! So there!

Anyway, I became a nurse. And it has been the best decision of my life. I learned to throw myself into my work, my patients and their well-being. That took away the time I would use to think about relationships or more specifically—the lack thereof.

This morning, I had the opportunity to see the true love I had hoped I would experience in this life. A couple who had been married for 53 years came to the Surgicentre; he was having a routine procedure. They still looked at each other with their eyes locked and a palpable emotion that everyone could see. She sat by his side, holding his hand, answering questions posed to him when he gave the slightest hesitation of recalling the information and smoothing his eyebrows with a tiny bit of her saliva. He was 73 years old, three years older than his wife—but interacted with her like a schoolboy with his first crush. As we went to roll him into the operating room, after she leant over and kissed him, he quickly reached out and pulled her closer saying, "You have made this life worth living. You are all that has ever really mattered to me."

"Just go, have that old appendix taken out, Joe!" she said, "You should have done it forty years ago!" They both laughed.

And I've been in a funk ever since.

I want to love and to be loved. I never was the girl that guys just looked at and knew they liked me; I was the one they thought they liked once they got to know me. Then, as luck would have it, one or both of us would realise that was not the case and they really didn't like me at all. Not until after the break-up anyway. After I have used every tactic known to any human to get over them, then they realised, "Oh, I really do like her!" But I decided a long time ago to never backtrack. I'm the same person I was in the beginning. If you didn't love/like me then, chances are you don't love/like me now.

Some women don't seem to have those issues. Take one of my best friends, Greta, for instance.

Greta was visibly beautiful, not just to men, but women recognised it as well. She did not really need makeup and barely ever wore any except mascara and clear lip gloss. Her skin was as clean and clear as a new-born's, never having had even the smallest pimple. She never had a weight problem, had great taste in apparel, and she had *good hair*. While she could not pass, it was clear by looking at her that she was likely bi-racial. Greta was never between relationships; she was just waiting to become available for the next guy waiting.

She had just graduated from George Washington University with her BS in Business when the four of us met nine years ago at a Zumba class. She put herself through school, working at Calibri's Italian Eatery, up in northwest, charming everyone she met and raking in tips hand over fist. She still works there, but now, as an assistant manager.

It was there that she met Cameron. He replaced the previous manager, and while orienting him to his new position, Greta and Cameron became fast friends, and lovers soon thereafter. It's been a year and a half, and they are still together.

Cameron, on the other hand, had never quite been loved the way he believed he deserved to be loved. Perhaps it was because he was the fifth consecutive son born to parents desperately wanting a girl from the start. His parents had billed him as the last chance for a daughter and decided that if Cameron was not a girl, they would quit trying. Interestingly enough, a post-partum night of comforting turned to unplanned passion and his parents got the girl they had always wanted nine months after Cameron was born. Cameron was destined to be overshadowed and overlooked from the moment his sister Stassi was brought home.

As he grew older, he developed a close relationship with Remy Martin Cognac. And by the time he was 31, Remy had ushered him to or saw him through many broken relationships and three divorces. After his last divorce, he threw in the towel. He swore off marriage and vowed that he would never try it again.

Of course, that's when he met Greta.

Cameron had become tame since meeting her. He gave up drinking, found his faith and is working hard to be a better man. He became a mentor for young men with absent fathers and learned that what he really wanted more than anything else was a child of his own. He wanted to be a father. Maybe, the one he never had.

He and Greta had had this conversation many, many times before. He wanted a child but not a marriage. Greta had never married, though she had come close a few years back. She wanted a family—but *absolutely* not without marriage. She wanted to be a wife. This morning it had come up again…

Cameron sat at the foot of the bed. He watched Greta as she stood in front of the mirror and pulled her long, curly black hair into a high ponytail. He watched her hair as it dropped and came to rest just above her buttocks. Their eyes met in the mirror, and Cameron shook his head.

"I don't know how my saying 'I don't want to get married' equals 'I don't love you'. I just don't get it," he said.

Greta turned around to look at him, "And I don't know why I have to keep telling you over and over again, Cameron. I am not having a baby before I get married! And I know that I love you. But do you even love me? When you truly love someone, you *want* to get married. You *want* to be a family in every way."

"There are many loving and happy couples with children who have never gotten married. Marriage is not a pre-requisite to having children anymore! This is not the fifties, Greta!"

"Well, it's a pre-requisite for me!" Greta exclaimed as she put on her lip gloss.

"Well, I've been there, done that and not so well," Cameron said, admitting defeat.

"Not with me, and you know that's what I want," she lamented.

Interrupting, "You know I don't want to get married again! I do not want to get married again!" he reiterated. "And yes, I really do want to be a dad." He pondered momentarily, then added, "You know how much I want a child. I could say that you don't love me!"

"You could, but you know that's not true, Cam!"

"And how do I know that?" he shot back quickly. "Why do you get to be the one that we *know* loves the other one? All I really know is you are so into yourself that you don't want to mess with that perfect body! It might keep some random guy from looking at you!"

"Jealousy is not a good look on you, Cam. You are going to want to stop talking before you go too far."

Cameron looked down at his bare feet resting on the white plush carpet as he sat off the foot of their California King and shook his head again. Almost inaudibly, he said, "I'm sick of this." He took a deep breath. He had given thought to it before. Not his first time at this rodeo, and the ride was rough and taking its toll.

"You know what, you're right," he said. "As a matter of fact, I don't think we should ever have this conversation again. I won't ever bring it up, and I'm asking you to never bring up marriage or children. When it comes up again, it has to be because one of us has decided to do something different. Because you know what? I can't do this anymore. I just can't!" he said with exhausted candour.

He stood and walked to the door, put his hand on the knob then stopped and looked back at stunned Greta.

"And I really do love you," he said honestly, then headed out of the door.

Greta was unable to respond; these conversations had now taken a new turn. This certainly meant a shift in the relationship—but to what end. She wondered…

Okay, back to me and why I am really in this funk.

Well, last night I dreamed about a superhero. I dreamed I was at work and a million things were happening, and I kept glancing around, in the midst of the chaos, looking for a superhero. Somehow, I knew he was coming, and I was waiting and looking for him with almost a desperation. Suddenly, I looked up, and there he was. All I could do was sigh in great relief and say, "My superhero!" Of course, then I woke up—so I don't know what else happened.

But I was quite perplexed when I woke up this morning, thinking about how tough my job must be if I subconsciously believe the only thing to help is a superhero! I called my baby sister Melissa and told her about the dream. She said I wasn't dreaming about the job, rather a man, a relationship. One thing for certain, he would have to be a real *superhero* to get my attention away from everything that surrounds what I do every day. And when I get home, all I care to do is a reboot!

But then, maybe I am waiting for some superhuman guy and I am either ignoring it or too stupid to know that I am.

My name is Giselle, I am now 49 years old and single. Harry and I have been divorced for 30 years, and as it turned out—he did know how to be in a loving relationship and treat a woman right. Truth is, we were both good people. Just not good together. For the past 30 years, I have thrown myself into my career, and I thrive on taking care of other people. But I haven't been in a serious relationship since that time.

My leisure time that I rarely carve out is spent with my girls Gabrielle (Gabby) and Greta, who you met earlier. We call ourselves the "G Squad". You know—Giselle, Gabby, Greta… And fair warning, this is not a man-bashing book. Just a conversation about myself and my girlfriends and some situations we encountered while just living. We used to call ourselves "three Gs and a B". But our friend Bridget succumbed to breast cancer three years ago.

Bridget was 38 years old and her demise was rapid. When she noticed a lump in her left breast, she refused to have it checked out. She did not tell anyone, not even a physician. Her mother, aunt and a sister had all succumbed to breast cancer. She had no desire for chemo, hair loss, nor the scent of death that haunted her through three deaths of people she loved. Every year since her death, the G Squad has run/walked the race for the cure at 'The Four Seasons' to raise money for a breast cancer.

Standing here right now in the outer lobby of this hotel in this pink tank top printed "3 Gs for a B" and while waiting for two other Gs dressed the same as me sort of pissed me off because they were late! They were always late! Always have been. Always will be. I caught a glimpse of myself in a mirrored window and looked away as soon as I realised I was looking at myself. I've always had to work hard to not weigh 200 pounds and just never liked seeing myself. Today was especially uneasy in these spandex pink, black and white swirled pants. Plus, I'm not so light on the booty side of things. But not a curvaceous beautiful butt, just a big butt! Anyway...

"Hey, G!" I heard Greta's voice calling out from behind me with a lot of morning cheer in her voice (and as though she was on time!).

"Good morning, G!" I said. I was happy she was there because I hate waiting. I really hate waiting anywhere alone especially when other people, with people—are laughing and having a great time.

"You know," I said, "I don't even know what I would do if anybody was ever, anywhere on time!" We gave each other a quick hug and suddenly felt someone else joining the embrace... Gabby had made it too.

Gabby had the perfect man, and her life was completely on track. She had been with Travis since high school and through college, when they started living together in their senior year. Gabby came from a simple middle-class family. Hard workers and no skeletons. God-fearing, churchgoers, who valued others, helping others and treating everybody right. And she was alright. No complaints. Not needing something better.

Travis was a generous man from both a poor and then quite a wealthy family. His parents were farmers who really struggled in the early years. But as they held on, the farm grew and eventually won two very lucrative contracts before establishing their own food line that proved tremendously successful nationwide. Travis had always planned on opening a Soup Kitchen for the homeless. That is where his heart lived, as he remembered the old days when his family really struggled.

Gabby met Travis when her family moved back to town after her mother left the military. They were both surprised to learn that they were born on the same day, the same year in the same hospital. They fell in love at age 13, officially "*going steady*" by 16 and never looked back. They went to the same college where Travis had a double major in Business and Agriculture, and Gabby got her BS in Social Work.

After living together for more than six years and on their 27th birthday, Travis popped the question. Not a lot of fanfare. Simply "Marry me" at a baseball game, not on the jumbotron, but sitting in the nosebleed section with a hotdog and beer. Gabby could not have wanted it any different. Together, they decided on a winter wedding.

While looking for wedding venues, they happened upon an empty and somewhat rundown building, that would clearly be a perfect space for a soup kitchen. Travis instantly knew that this was the place and began the process of purchasing the building. Gabby was included on everything legally and in the decision-making process, because they shared the same desire of giving and helping others as a life's work. This was their life, and it was beautiful.

Fast forward to December 17. Gabby and Travis' wedding day on the 20th. An idiot driving fast on a slippery icy road took Travis' life on his way home from work. Gabby was beyond devastated. Yet she knew that she wanted his legacy to live on. He left her 1.23 million dollars. She purchased the building and *Travis' Kitchen* was born. Fully dedicated to feeding and helping the homeless and others wanting or needing a hot meal. That was eight years ago.

Gabby is soon to be 36 and has yet to love another man. Gabby had never been with any man other than Travis her entire life, and it was not something that interested her. In a strange way, it seemed he had never left her. Besides—she was always surrounded by family or friends, and her vibrator was awesome.

As we went inside to register for the race, I noticed Greta was not quite there.

I bumped her shoulder with mine, "What's up, G?"

She laughed it off. Probably because just as I bumped her, it was her turn to sign in and the gentleman calling her over was very easy on the eyes. Suddenly, Greta came alive and whatever may have been bothering her evaporated.

We slow-walked the race, crossing the finish line at 1:53:33, then headed out to brunch. After a few mimosas, we were laughing and talking about Bridget and her crazy antics. Bridget was always the comedian of the group. "I always get tickled," I said, "thinking about when we were being followed around Kessler's (a very high-end Department Store) as if we were going to shoplift."

"Yeah! Bridget reversed the tables and started following HIM!" Gabby said with a chuckle.

"Look at him," Gabby said using her Bridget voice and facies, "he's following us. Come on." Beckoning us to follow, then slowly walking toward him and standing next to him while looking through the lady's clothes rack!

"And she stayed until he felt uncomfortable and moved away while keeping us in his sight. Bridget kept dragging us behind her as we followed him from rack to rack, all the while laughing at the fact that he was uncomfortable!" I said, just tickled all over again!

Laughing so hard she could hardly get her words out, Gabby blurted, "But the kicker was when Bridget whispered to him 'Sir, I'm done looking in the lady's section. I don't see anything I want. But I'm also looking for a tie for my husband. Would you go to the men's department next so I can see what you have there? We would really rather follow you' then scanning the room, looking back to him and whispering— 'you know, so you can be sure that we don't steal anything.' And sarcastically nodded her head! He just turned red and walked away!"

"From that day forward, that was our thing when we went to any department store and were profiled; we reversed the tables and just followed them," I added.

Bridget was very comfortable in her blackness. She went natural before natural hair was trendy and was Afrocentric in her style of dress. She had visited Africa twice before she got sick. "Every black person needs to visit the Motherland at least once in their life," she would say. Finally, she convinced us all to take the girls trip of our lives to Africa. Much to our dismay, on the last day of our trip, we found that it was to make the big reveal about her terminal cancer. We knew something was wrong closer to the end. We questioned. She denied. It took the beauty of Africa to give her the courage to tell us quietly in the most beautiful sunset I've ever seen in my life. I haven't cried that much since.

Three months after Africa, Bridget died.

After brunch and talking about Bridget, I began to feel sombre. Apparently, Greta had texted Cameron, because he showed up to pick her up. Gabby and I followed her out and left as well.

When he arrived, Cameron had a box of chocolates and one long stem pink rose waiting in the passenger seat. He was standing, waiting to open the door for her. She came directly to him and kissed him as though she had not seen him in two weeks. They then held each other for a few more moments. "I love you," she said.

"I love you too," he said, reluctant to let go of her.

Cameron reached for the handle and opened the car door. When Greta saw the box of chocolates and the pink rose (which Cameron knew was her favourite flower), she turned and kissed him again.

Seemed they could not get home soon enough. They were hugging and kissing, and he worked to unlock the door while never letting go. She was straddling him as he carried her into the bedroom during a long, continuous kiss all the time reaching to caress him...

They struggled to undress because neither of them wanted to let go of the other. His tongue on her body was only made more intense when his tongue entered her body.

Chapter 2

Sunday morning, and here we go! I could not even understand! The woman looked so angry this morning and her husband was clinging so closely to her and cowering a bit. My God! Okay, here's the story…

We were in church. I always catch the 7 am service because it leaves the rest of the day to do as I please. Well, I found my favourite place to sit a long time ago—the 6th pew on the left end. There were others who sat on the same pew, who also had their specific areas of the pew to sit. For the first couple of years, as we settled into our respective seating areas, everything was fine. I'd sit on my end, a married couple would sit at the opposite end, or in some region of our bench, with the husband closer to me but not too close and his wife on the other side of him. Random others would come and go, sometimes sitting between us or on the end. I was always on time, so I always had my end, but basically, you could count on myself and the couple as the regulars.

Well, about eight months ago after the *miracle prayer*, in the middle of hand-holding, she made her husband switch places with her, gave me a super mad look and she sat on the inside of our trio since. For the past four or five months, she had become gradually less friendly toward me. When the pastor would say, "Look at your neighbour and say… whatever…" if it's my turn for us to look and interact with each other, she would look down at her shoes and lean and wipe something off them or just look forward when he would say, "turn to your other neighbour…" She did not participate on the member level with me at all lately. She had started to leave for whatever reason when it was time to hold hands and return afterwards. They even left sometimes before benediction when there was no one between us.

I had started to feel a little bad, trying to figure out what I had done. Or even what she thought that I had done. We knew nothing of each other. We had no connection other than church. But she won't let me high five her or tell her what pastor says. And the way they looked on this Sunday, I had nothing good coming.

To add insult to injury, it was just announced that our pastor was not preaching. Instead, someone from the ministerial staff was going to bring the message. I felt like getting up going home.

Lord, I know I need to be here. I am happy to hear Your word—but I love hearing the word from my pastor! Lord, forgive me, I thought.

The truth was, it bothered me more than a little bit, this disdain from my pew neighbour. I just didn't get that. I might as well get up then. Looking behind me, pew 7 was empty on the end. There was a member who usually sits there, and she was not there yet. I didn't want to take her seat, but...

The devil is so busy! Really? Am I having this conversation with myself right now, in the church no less, instead of giving my Lord God Almighty praise, honour and thanks? Really Giselle?

Jesus, help me...

I refuse to let other people affect my church experience. I need it to survive, I thought.

Arriving home, I decided I just wanted to binge-watch *Cheers, (yes – Cheers!)* on Netflix. After being reduced to high fiving myself in church, I needed a laugh! But next Sunday, that was not going to be a problem because I was giving up the 6th pew. My spirituality was more important than a favourite seat in the church.

The light bulb blew as soon as I turned it on inside my closet. I forgot trying to hang up my church clothes. That made about five light bulbs out in that condo right then (Yes! five!). I knew I must replace them. Or soon I would be walking around in complete darkness! I was going to put on a pair of sweats and head to Lowes. I really hate doing handyman chores. I hate changing light bulbs, taking out the trash, any kind of outdoor and lawn work you can think of. I just hate it. Therefore, it took five light bulbs blowing before I decided to replace them.

Oh well, here goes...

Travis' Kitchen always served a full sit-down Sunday meal from 11:45 in the morning to 7:30 pm. Gabby arrived at 7 am today, because she had just hired a new cook, Oliver, and today was his first day on the job. Oliver had been very impressive during his interview, and she hired him on the spot. There was something about him that struck her in a way that compelled her to believe in him. As she headed to the door this morning, she saw her new employee sitting at the front door stoop.

Early.

She liked that.

Oliver had his long, blond, somewhat curly hair pulled back into a low ponytail, and his blue eyes were bright and anxious. His white chef's coat, still in the cleaner's cellophane bag was draped across his arm, and he stood to greet her. His face was clean-shaven but carried the wear of worry on it. He had always worked hard and dreamed of being a renowned chef with a Michelin star restaurant and impossible to get reservations. But it never happened for him. Yet he never gave up. He answered her ad, and so it began.

"Good morning," he said, extending his hand.

"Good morning," she answered back. "You're really early," Gabby said, somewhat inquisitive as to why. "An hour and a half, in fact!"

"I know. I wanted to really get a good look at the layout of the whole kitchen. I wanted to see what I needed and have a chance to present you with options for today's meal and maybe even figure out what we're doing for the rest of the week."

Gabby stepped past him and unlocked the door. He followed, looking behind them and closing the door.

"I think that was a really good idea," Gabby said while turning the lights on, "coming in early. Says a lot about you."

"Good things, I hope," Oliver answered with a slight smile.

"Very good things!" she said. She then showed him around the kitchen and left him to explore the vast pantry and walk-in refrigerator and freezers.

Within an hour, he was knocking on her office door, completely thrilled with the whole set up, most especially the fresh vegetables and herbs. He felt alive as though he could put a special spin on soup kitchen dining.

"Come in," she said.

"Hey, I've had a good look around and, uh…wow! This place is phenomenal! You have everything here!" Oliver exclaimed.

"I know. We have a lot of volunteer support from the community and kind of our own farm," Gabby said, looking back down to her computer and entering data. "We've been really fortunate to get a lot of financial support from the community as well. So, what did you come up with?"

"Well, I was hoping to do two entrees. A nice garden salad, Chicken and Eggplant parmesan, asparagus, homemade yeast rolls and double chocolate brownies."

"For at least 400 people? You might want to pace yourself. Have you ever cooked for huge groups of people?"

"Well, I didn't think I would be doing it alone. What's my team like again?"

"We have volunteers—six for the first six hours starting at eight and dropping to three until we close at 7:00, as other volunteers come and go," Gabby said.

She looked up and added, "You are the only paid staff in the kitchen. I'm happy to see your enthusiasm, Oliver—but maybe meatloaf and potatoes to start. The prep work is done already—okay?"

"Fair enough…" Oliver looked at her for a moment as though he wanted to say something else. But decided to nod and leave the office.

As I searched feverishly, looking for the correct fricking light bulbs, I was again reminded that I was a single woman. I didn't like to think about it really. I accepted some time ago that I will never be one of those women with the forever love story. I was almost certainly over halfway through my life. And so far, I'd had nothing near it. I was never going to have the man who looks into my eyes and sees my soul, all the hurt and disappointments, the joy and the laughter, the hopes and the dreams—the real me—and love what he sees. I had been through great pain, accepted that I would not be one of those women who gets flowers at work for no reason or who finds love notes before going to work in the morning. And I was reminded of all of this just because of a damn light bulb! Well, five light bulbs…

Then a manly arm reached past me, brushing my arm as he easily picked the perfect light bulb *he's* looking for, as though he made them. "Excuse me." I said feeling a bit disrespected.

He said, "Excuse me," then looked at me and smiled. Now he's off to replace the bulbs for his lovely wife or perfect girlfriend!

Heeeyyyyyyy! I think I may be *bitter*! This is the reason I don't like buying light bulbs!

But he was really someone I could see myself with for some reason. The way he looked at me for like a split second just seemed familiar.

Okay, back to reality.

I really hate replacing light bulbs. Next time, I'm going get one of those handyman apps or something. Anyway, I picked three 2-packs and headed to check out. I accidentally dropped my credit card on the floor and bent to pick it up. Naturally, when I stood, I found myself eye to eye with guess who? The 'light bulb man'!

I don't know why but I felt something inside of me moving emotionally and my heart jumping just a little bit as our eyes met. I was almost startled looking into his eyes. We both instinctively looked away. I paid for the fricking light bulbs and went home.

Chapter 3

Every other Monday morning, fresh vegetables and dairy products were delivered to the kitchen from Travis' family farm. Lately, the newly hired driver, Calvin, had been coming on stronger and stronger to Gabby. She thought very little of his advances and had just been ignoring him for the past few months—which did not appear to do anything but make him try harder.

Strangely enough, when she heard the truck this morning, she got up and checked her hair and face in the mirror. She quickly caught herself and shook her head while continuing to look at herself in the mirror.

Gabby was fairly certain that Calvin had no idea of the connection she had with Travis' family. And even though it had been eight years, his parents still treated her like family, and it really mattered to her what they might think of her. Spending time with Calvin was never an option or a desire. But she was finding their harmless banter refreshing.

Oliver was doing prep work in the back. She got his attention by tapping on the steel table, "Hey, the truck's here. Come, see, you'll be doing this from now on. It comes every other Monday."

Oliver took off his apron, washed his hands and headed to the back door and stood next to Gabby.

Two men got out of the truck, headed to the back and started to unload the fresh, boxed products. The first one to bring a box said, "Hello, beautiful."

Laughing, Gabby responded, "Calvin." Indicating Oliver, she added, "Meet Oliver, our new chef."

Calvin nodded, and Oliver did the same. Oliver then assisted to unload the truck and watched Gabby as she finished the transaction with a school-girl type giddiness at Calvin's persistent flirtations.

Calvin was not a great looking guy. No great body. Obviously, he had no real money—was a working man. He seemed to only live for the moment, and he had never really been serious in any of their interactions. But he had *spice.* He had confidence, and he knew how to be charming. He also knew he was wearing Gabby down.

After the final product was unloaded and stored, (Travis' family ensured that Gabby never had to do the work of storing or hiring someone to stock the delivery. They provided the muscle in Travis' absence), Calvin eased over to Gabby's side and sang harmoniously, "Good morning, Gabrielle!"

Gabby tilted her head to indicate that she was not impressed.

Calvin intimately spoke, saying, "Is today the day that you are finally going to bless me? Is today the day that you are going to make me the happiest man alive?" and again sang, "Miss Gabrielle!" with a huge smile on his face and moving even closer.

Gabby straight-armed him away from her. "You know, Calvin, one day I may just say yes just to watch you squirm!"

"I never squirm, baby!" Calvin said, then leant and whispered into her ear, "But I know I can make you squirm and love every minute of it!"

"Not today, mister!" Gabby quick-stepped away from him. "See you next Monday, Romeo!"

Calvin caught her before she could get away and pressed a piece of paper into the palm of her hand.

Gabby looked at the paper. Seeing his phone number, she said, "You've given this to me twice before already, you know!"

"Of course, I know!" he said, "I'm going to keep giving it to you until you use it!" He flashed a great smile, then headed out of the back door.

Gabby, clearly affected, closed the door, smiling broadly while shaking the paper with Calvin's number written on it.

Oliver had been paying attention to Gabby from the moment Calvin arrived. He instantly saw the difference in Gabby and just shook his head and laughed a little bit to himself.

Gabby saw him...

Puzzled and maybe a bit dismayed—Gabby asked, "What's that supposed to mean?"

"Nothing," he said, still shaking his head and sighing, as if to say—surely, you recognise this is game, and lame game at that!

"What!" she semi-shouted.

"He's not sincere, you know," Oliver said earnestly. "He's just trying to see how far he can get. Running game."

Gabby was full-blown agitated at that point. "And how do you know how sincere he is? What makes you the expert? Are you a relationship expert? And what makes you think I want him to be serious at this point?"

"I'm just saying is all..." Oliver said, fading back into his prep work.

"Do you even know me well enough to say that to me? You barely know me 13 minutes and you're giving me life advice?"

Oliver stopped and looked at Gabby. "I did not give you any life advice! You asked me what I was thinking, and against my better judgement, I told you! But you can't handle it. Don't ask the question if there's a possibility that you can't stand the answer!"

"You know what, Oliver? Why don't you just pay attention to the kitchen and your cooking? Not to me and my life—even if I ask! Do you think you can do that?" She left the kitchen, heading to her office mumbling angrily, "The nerve of that guy!"

Oliver had really struck a chord. Not so much because he could be right, but because Gabby had not given the first thought to Calvin's intentions. And she had found herself enjoying it. But the fact was, it wasn't Oliver's business anyway!

Greta and Cameron had been operating on a cooler level since the Race for the Cure Saturday argument. It had been more than two weeks since it happened, and even though they made up and made love, there was an unusual element now living in their relationship. Not only at home or when they were alone, but there were noticeable changes in his behaviour at work as well. Today, they did not ride into work together or back home. He had to 'work late'.

Greta wasn't sure of what was happening to them, but she knew it wasn't good. She also knew that she still loved him, more than ever, in fact. And she didn't want to lose him. She asked herself if maybe she was being ridiculous. She knew Cameron's life, his experiences and what had made him who he was. And was she setting herself up to lose him? She had known well before that Saturday, that Cameron wanted a child and she had stopped taking her birth control nearly four months before. But she had not shared that with him.

She decided it was still too soon to mention this to Cameron. She must be certain first. She heard him loud and clear when he said neither of them was to bring up marriage or babies until they had changed their perspective on the impasse. She could do that. And she could really feel herself changing and loving him more and more. Yet, she was afraid as she had not been before, that he was leaving her.

The disconnect between them had lingered for a couple of more weeks. Greta knew at some point there had to be a conversation.

When Cameron got home, he was clearly preoccupied. Greta felt uncomfortable. She was hesitant to ask him what was wrong. She wasn't sure that she wanted to know. It might open a can of worms she wasn't ready to face and possibly could not close again. That being the case, she still had to say something.

"Hey, babe," she said, "you okay?"

"Hey," he quietly answered. "I'm good."

She walked over to him and initiated an embrace. They both held each other so tight, with love and passion. "I love you, Cam."

"I love you too, baby," he said. "But I think we need to talk."

Cameron took Greta's hand and led her to the sofa and seated her. She felt her heart sink when he left her there, walked across the room and gazed out of their large glass window. He took a deep breath, placed both hands on the glass and dropped his head, which landed on the glass as well.

"Cameron, you're scaring me," Greta barely squeaked out.

Without turning around, Cameron said, "I think Race Saturday was the hardest day of my life since I've been sober. I had to fight off the urge to drink, and it was strong." He turned and looked at Greta but leant his back against the window glass.

He continued, "I've been thinking a lot since then. I am not a perfect man. I don't know." He shook his head and looked down, then back to Greta. "Even though it has been, I guess, a month, I find myself crushed because of myself. I love you, Greta. I love you." He repeated it a third time with even more feelings and emotions, "I love you. And I think it took Saturday to make me realise that I am being unfair to you. I can't expect you to give up your beliefs for me. You deserve someone who can and will give you everything you want."

Greta shook her head, interrupting, "No, Cam. I don't like where this is going. Don't do this…"

"Greta, please let me finish…" Cameron continued, not moving an inch from the window.

Tears started to well up in Greta's eyes, and she held her head back as if that will stop them from flowing. She knew.

"You deserve it all, Greta," Cameron continued. "You've helped me find my life again, and I will always be thankful to you for that. You believed in me when no one else did, and that made me believe in myself again. But I'm such a failure. I've failed at three marriages, and I'm barely 33 years old!"

"Cam—" Greta attempted to interrupt.

"No, Greta, let me finish!" He took another deep breath, "I promised myself I would never ever get married again. You deserve better than that, and I refuse to keep you in that position."

Greta dropped her head into her hands. She had seen the writing on the wall. She started to sob audibly.

Cameron walked over to her, got down on both knees in front of her and attempted to remove her hands from her face while saying, "I'm sorry, Greta. I'm sorry for ever putting you in this position. I was wrong, and I'm sorry. Greta, look at me…"

She did not look up. She continued the same.

"Greta, please look at me. Please…" Cameron begged. "Greta," he said in a very quiet and comforting voice, "please look at me."

Greta raised her head, and through the massive tears in her eyes, she saw the most perfectly round French Pave' Diamond engagement ring, platinum, ideal cut about three carats and costing nearly fifty thousand dollars. She knew this ring! She had sort of joked with Cameron about it a few months back. He told her, "You can file that under it's never going to happen!"

Greta could not speak.

But Cameron could—"How could you ever think I would let you go? I love you. And loving you makes me happy for everything I've been through in my entire life—my parents, addiction, failures, divorces, even my low self-esteem—if that was the path I needed to take to get to you, then it was all worth it. I will never need or want more than you. Never."

Cameron repositioned himself to kneeling on one knee.

"Greta, will you marry me?"

It took her a moment, but she realised what she thought was going to be the worst moment of her life, turned out to be the best. Greta started to laugh, "Yes! Yes! Yes!"

They kissed.

Greta punched Cameron in the chest. "I should have said no for what you just put me through!"

Laughing and grabbing her fist, "I didn't see it going that way! That was not the plan!" Cameron responded.

Chapter 4

For some crazy reason, I kept thinking about the light bulb man. It's very rare when someone grabs my attention and holds it—unintentionally—which means it's all me, by the way!

There was just something about him that seemed to awaken this long since asleep libido. I thought about him at the most random times. I could see his green eyes looking into me, as though he could see my soul, the deepest parts of me, the part that wanted and needed to live again, to love again, to make love again and not with an inanimate object! Seemed the light bulb man had really turned me on. But to what end for me?

Greta called and invited me for drinks at Colby's in an hour. She said she just wanted to hang out "briefly". She'd been acting weird lately. From time to time, she mentioned Cameron and that he's acting weird. Thank God for relationship people! Every time I started to think that I want one, they helped me to realise that I do not! Gabby was going to be there too. That probably meant Greta wanted to share something significant.

So, I was getting a quick shower. I didn't really want to go, but I guessed I would. Sometimes, I just don't want to hang out. I want to hang in! I was listening to the evening news from the shower and I heard something about a four-alarm fire. I left the bathroom with just a towel and caught the news in the event it might affect my commute.

The reporter asked if the cause of the fire had been determined, and there was suddenly a close-up of Kevin Harper, Deputy Fire Chief—AKA—The light bulb man!

"Not yet. But of course, we will continue to investigate. Eight families have been displaced, but miraculously, there were no fatalities so far," he said.

I just stood there. Stunned, with a towel. Watching this interview. Of the light bulb man aka Kevin Harper, Deputy Fire Chief. In his uniform. Saving lives. Putting out fires. Interviewing. Live. On the evening news. Well, there you have it!

Really? Really, life?

I sat on the edge of the bed and watched the news until the next story came on. And then just a little longer. You see at first, the haunting only consisted of his rude but slightly desired touch, his green eyes and a random meeting at the checkout counter. Now I have a name, an awesome occupation and an ever so real person. The man who has been invading my thoughts for weeks now, Kevin Harper, Deputy Fire Chief—AKA—the light bulb man.

Lord, help me…What is going on in the universe right now? I thought.

I arrived at Colby's 20 minutes late, and guess what? I was the first one there! They make me so sick! Just once you would think they would be someplace on time. I should have just stayed in the car, waited until they got here and made them wait. But I decided that I wouldn't.

I was seated at a table near the window so I could see the entrance of the parking lot. But I was also positioned so I could see the door.

My God, they make me sick. I hate waiting!

I'm not a big fan of drinking, but I wanted something. I thought about a mimosa (okay! I'm not a big drinker!) while I waited. I was nearly a full mimosa in when Gabby showed up.

"Is that a mimosa?" Gabby questioned.

"It is. And?" I asked quite defensively in fact. "I can have a mimosa."

"I know you can. But I also know you rarely ever take a drink of any sort! What's up with you?" she asked.

The waitress came over, and Gabby requested a 'Raspberry Iced Tea'.

"You mean a Long Island Iced Tea, right?" I meddled with a chuckle.

"No. I mean what I said."

"And you typically drink just to say you had a drink! It's like we are living in an alternate universe! Why tea this evening?"

She gave some thought, then said, "I don't know. I feel like I don't need to drink right now. I want to have a clear mind when I go back to the Kitchen and fire Oliver."

"Wait, what?" I was caught off-guard. "Why are you firing Oliver? You said he was a very good chef, very organised, very helpful and just great for the Kitchen. What gives?"

"I know I said that, and all of it is true," she admitted, "but he's weird, and I feel like he's judging me or something all of the time. He looks at me like I disappoint him or something. It's really weird."

"Okay, I don't get it," I said.

"I don't get it either!" Gabby declared. "But yesterday we had a real argument about Calvin! Calvin! Of all things to argue about!" I frowned, trying to figure out who Calvin was. "You know! The product delivery guy!"

"Oh, yeah!"

"Well, Calvin was big-time flirting with me, like he always does, and Oliver was like, 'he's trying to run games on you!' It was crazy to me, and it really pissed me off!"

I was putting two and two together. "Is Oliver attracted to you?"

"No!" Gabby blurted quickly. Then she became a bit pensive. "I don't think so." She considered the possibility, then shook her head. "Nope. He's not attracted to me. He's just a pain in my butt; that's all!"

We both took a sip of our drinks, and Gabby looked at me again, asking, "So what's up with you and Mimosas on this fine evening?"

"Nothing but work, my friend," I said, beckoning for our waitress and raising my glass when she looked at me. "I don't have time for anything else. Not to mention that I don't need any drama in my life. Work is more than enough."

"And what about love?" Gabby prodded. "You know at some point you're going to want to have some love in your life, maybe a little or a lot of sex in your life! When are you going to at least give it some thought?"

"Gabby, please don't start that today!"

I just hate it when people ask me questions like that. As if I can just order up the man I want in my life, like an evening mimosa at Colby's. If he was available to me and wanted me AND I wanted him at the same time, we would already be together.

"I don't need any of that, thank you," I said. "All I need is to go to work and pay my bills. I'm okay with whatever else happens! But thanks anyway!"

I had not told Gabby or Greta about the light bulb man AKA Kevin Harper, Deputy Fire Chief. And I wasn't about to open myself up to their scrutiny today about my love life—or lack thereof. Besides, I was already tripping. All I needed was their input to tip me fully off the scale!

"There's Greta AND Cameron!" I said.

Gabby looked around. "Is he coming in too? What's that all about?"

"No," I said, "he's going back to the car. Did he just walk her to the restaurant door, open it, let her in and go back to his fricking car? Really? What is he trying to make up for?"

"Wow!" Gabby said.

I waved to Greta, and she headed our way.

Greta kept her hand in her pockets; she wanted a grand entrance for her star.

"What's up, Gs?" she asked, again happily presenting herself as though she was on time!

"What are you guys drinking? Giselle! Is that a mimosa?"

"My second no less!" I bragged.

"And I guess that's your second Long Island Iced Tea? Huh?" she asked Gabby.

"I'll have you know this is 'Raspberry Iced Tea'! No alcohol at all!" Gabby proudly answered.

"Geeze! What's wrong with this picture?" Greta laughed. She kept her hands in her pockets while ordering lemon wedges and water. "What's up with you, guys?" She asked, trying to hold in her excitement. But it was driving her crazy! She was smiling from ear to ear.

I had to ask her, "You know the television commercials where a person with horrible teeth get new ones in one day? Well, you're smiling like the after picture right now! Spill!"

Greta took her left hand out of her pocket and slammed it palm down on the table exposing her beautifully exquisite engagement ring. "3.1 carats!" she said, nodding her head. "Cameron asked me to marry him!"

Bombshell!

So, we all screamed and congratulated her. We discussed dates and wedding themes. We considered venues and destination weddings, and we all enjoyed the happiness of her engagement to the man she loved, and we knew he loved her as well. But I started to drift away…

I started to think of how I really did want a man in my life. I wanted to love and to be loved. Then my uncooperative brain took me back to *Maybe I'm just not that girl. Maybe I'm not the girl who gets a happy ending.* I was realistic and not prone to fantasising. But I wondered about him sometimes. I wondered if he did exist. Was there a man out there for me? Someone who was searching for me just as I was searching for him. Someone who could only be completed by me, just as only I could complete him. Was the same one that I needed so much, out there somewhere needing me just as much? But most of all, was I going to recognise him and be open to receive him when he comes? Was it possible that my someone was going to be *super* enough to love me right? And can he find me and I find him? I was really tripping!

Well, they say when you are ready, the universe provides what you need. I knew that I had not been open to a relationship and I didn't know that I was then. But there were two things that I did know and with great certainty. Number one, I was ready to go home; and number two, Cameron was compensating for something! I knew that ring. And you could buy a small BMW with what he paid for it!

Chapter 5

Gabby was a bit anxious going back to the Kitchen the next morning. She hadn't really talked to Oliver since the Calvin thing. They'd had small talk but even that felt awkward. She decided she would talk to him, clear the air and maybe gain some understanding of why the interaction had gone so far left field.

Three knocks on her office door.

"Come in."

Oliver stuck his head in the door. "Hey, you got a minute?"

"Sure, come on in," she said.

Oliver came in and closed the door behind himself. He then motioned to the chair, asking for permission to sit. Gabby nodded in agreement.

"I wanted to say," Oliver started off, "that I am sorry for that Monday thing. I didn't mean to offend you. But it's clear, to me anyway, that I did. I'm sorry. And I just wanted you to know that."

"I appreciate that, Oliver. I really do. But I don't understand where it came from. Why did you say those things?" she asked.

"Is it okay if I just say I'm sorry and we will not go through frames of mind and all of that? Sometimes, I see things differently from other people, and I already know my thoughts upset you."

With a slight laugh of disbelief and shaking her head, Gabby said, "Sometimes, Oliver, it feels like you are judging me. And I really don't like that. I don't need that in my life right now. And why do you even have *thoughts* about me and my life!"

Silence overtook the room.

Their eyes met, and they connected for a fleeting moment.

Oliver looked away and thought for a few seconds, then said, "I work hard to see everyone, to legitimately see people as individuals. Maybe it's because I went through a period where I felt unseen by anyone. I don't know." Deep sigh. "I am really sorry. But I don't mean to judge you at all. And if I'm not already fired, I probably will be after I tell you this. But if I'm being completely honest with you, I just don't think you realise what a wonderful person you are. I think you don't get that you make this crazy huge difference in the world. Not out of obligation but because that's who you are. What you do is so incredible, so amazing. I think you should just think about who you are and what you do here on this earth. Amazing!"

The honesty from Oliver had Gabby completely riveted. It took her voice away; she said nothing.

"I don't think he's good enough for you," he said earnestly, "and I don't want to see you hurt," Oliver added.

Taking a deep breath first, Gabby squeezed out, "And you think Calvin is going to hurt me?"

"I don't know that. But there's something very selfish and arrogant about him. I don't like him—and I like everybody!" he said, shaking his head. "I think you deserve better. There I go saying too much again. Sorry, again…" He shrugged one shoulder.

Gabby was unsure of how to react to this. "Well… thanks…I think. But I got this!"

Oliver stood but hesitated for a moment as though he was waiting to be fired or dismissed. The phone rang, and Gabby answered on the first ring. She maintained eye contact with Oliver, who waited.

"Calvin?" Gabby laughed. "How do you know I want to cook dinner for you tonight?" Gabby said, still maintaining eye contact with Oliver.

Oliver broke the eye contact with no obvious reaction and left the office, closing the door behind himself.

After the phone call, Gabby went to find Oliver. She felt his thoughts like daggers in her soul when he left the office, even though he showed no reaction. She wanted to see him. She had a morbid curiosity of what his reaction really was.

Oliver was standing in the walk-in refrigerator, admiring the beautiful mound of fresh vegetables when Gabby walked in. He turned and looked at her for a couple of seconds, then turned back at the veggies.

"I'm thinking about a beautiful fresh veggie chicken stew," he said. "Very hearty, thick, but white, no marinara or tomatoes—my special recipe. A side of cornbread and probably freshly brewed tea." He looked back at Gabby.

For a moment, when she first looked at him again, she again saw something. Something that she had been missing—for a fleeting moment. She stuttered a bit.

"So, what's the special recipe?"

Oliver reached up and took an apron off the wall. He then walked over and draped it around Gabby's neck and said, "How about you help me prep and I will show you my special recipe?" He took the apron strings, wrapped them around her back and tied them in the front of her as she offered no resistance.

"Okay," she said.

I think I'm kind of lost when it comes to romantic love. Ever since seeing the light bulb man AKA Kevin Harper, Deputy Fire Chief, I've been distracted. Now with Greta getting married, I was second-guessing all my romantic rejections from both sides, as well as every thought I had about relationships.

But let's be real here. What was the likelihood that at the age of 49, I would find this super and quite an elusive man? Even if he did exist, by this time I was sure he had more baggage than I did.

I am a very strong and independent woman. I had finished college, purchased my home and was well into my career before I was 25—on my own. I have always been a little bit on the thick side, but I've never been ugly—inside or out, I've always been attractive for the opposite sex. I could always *get* any man I wanted. Problem was, I just couldn't *keep* him.

Finally, I had been involved with so much *game* that I could recognise it within the first minute of a conversation. Then there were those who thought they loved me—but soon thereafter found out that they did not. Whether it was because they wanted to *mould* me into the way they saw me in their minds or *fold* me or make me bend over backwards for them or *scold* me for being me—they always seemed to find out they were in love with an idea of me—but never with me. Pretty soon, I found it much easier to say no from the start.

I poured myself into my job, and I became exceedingly good at it. I'm a nurse manager over a 20-suite hospital-based operating room. And I can assure you, I get all the emotions, the highs and lows, the love and hate, the disdain and the admiration of an actual relationship at the same place that pays for me to maintain a lifestyle with one job that is difficult to maintain on a two-salary income for most people.

So fast forward to now. I hadn't been in a real relationship for nearly thirty years. Wow! It scared *me* when I said that out loud. But I had been okay. For the most part, I'd been okay.

Until now that was! *Until the light bulb man! AKA Kevin Harper, Deputy Fire Chief!*

Truth was, I could control this! I refused to get fully distracted by a mirage that was highly likely to make me cry in the end. So, there you have it!

Chapter 6

A monthly mandatory meeting was a condition of employment for the whole Calibri's staff. The restaurant had been successful for over forty years. Growing with time and remaining a thriving community favourite by carefully choosing the staff and ensuring that they had a voice in certain decision-making arenas.

Breakfast was always provided because the meeting was always at 8:30 am. And an impressive spread was always made available. Greta had started early setting up the breakfast for the team and was finishing up, while Cameron was putting the finishing touches on the meeting's agenda.

Once Greta was done and the staff started to arrive, she went to the office to check on Cam's progress and see if he needed her to do anything.

"Hey," she said, "the gang's arriving. You've got about ten minutes. What do you need?"

"Oh, get the new uniforms out of the car and change into the blue one. They are hanging in the back behind the driver seat."

Cameron printed the agenda and ballots and quickly stapled the two sheets together. When Greta returned, with one set of solid royal blue and one set green, black and white plaid, they both took off the old uniforms' red vests and bow ties and exchanged them for the new ones, coordinating with the black crisply pressed slacks and sparkling white shirts.

In the private dining room, Greta and Cameron found that the staff had gathered. Most of them were already seated and having breakfast while some were still serving themselves at the buffet. Cameron tapped the podium and said, "Good morning, everyone. Let's take about three to five more minutes and get seated so we can start." He got himself a cup of coffee but passed on the full breakfast.

The meeting progressed fairly quickly. "Okay, only a couple of more things. I know you all have noticed what Greta and I are wearing, and yes, we are changing the uniforms a bit. We are keeping the white shirts and black slacks, but choosing new vests and ties."

Moans and groans and rumblings filled the room from the team.

One person asked, "Why do we have to change?"

Another added, "And who picked those colours!" There was some laughter in the room.

"Calm down," Cameron said. "These are the choices. You've had nearly an hour looking at both. So, you get to make the decision, or I will decide and hope most of you agree. There's a ballot attached to the agenda. Real simple. Circle Blue or Green. Real simple. Once you're done, give it to Greta."

"What's wrong with the red ones, Cameron?" someone asked, "I really like the red, it's my colour!"

"Well, let's just hope one of these is too!" Cameron laughed. "We need a facelift and little bump, something different. For now, this is it. And guys, choose carefully; we're all going to wear these for a while."

Greta collected the ballots. "Is this everyone?" she asked. "Is this it?" The team indicated "yes". Greta and Cameron came together to count as the team chattered and laughed while waiting.

Cameron tapped the podium again—"It's green!"

One loud "No!" came from the crowd, then a generalised splattering of applause and grunts.

"Well, it was really close. Blue lost by three votes," Cameron said. He then gave them a few seconds to absorb the results of the vote.

"Okay, one last thing," he said. "Let's get finished. But before I go to this, is there anything else anyone wants to bring up for discussion?"

"Can we stick with the red uniforms?" the same female voice asked, pleading.

Laughing, Cameron answered, "No. We cannot."

Cameron took a sip of his coffee, looked at Greta then back at the team.

"I've been very fortunate since being given the opportunity to manage Calibri's over two years ago," Cameron started. "I've had and still have the best team, the best customers and the absolute best love of my life," looking back at Greta, "as most of you already know." He paused and reflected, then added, "I am not a perfect man. Perfection doesn't seem to live in me. But I've found the perfect love to fit into my life, and she has assured me that I am the one to fit into hers. Greta has agreed to be my wife!" He took her hand and pulled her from her seat and lightly kissed her while the team cheered and offered congratulations.

Greta turned and flashed her ring for all to see from a distance amidst more cheers and ooohs and aahhs.

Cameron interrupted, "So listen up, Greta and I will be out, starting Thursday—"

Greta interrupted, "We will?" She looked surprised. "I didn't know that."

"I'm taking my fiancée on a 'thank you for saying yes weekend' to Niagara Falls," he said.

More wows and chatters from the team.

He continued, "And Tommy, I'm going to need you to cover, and we need to talk…"

A previously quiet waitress, Lisa, abruptly stood and said, "Oh my God! I think I'm going to throw up! I'm sorry, excuse me!" She sprinted out of the room toward the restrooms.

Cameron watched her as she cleared the room then almost as if it hadn't happened, continued, "Tommy, because you will be covering, we need to talk. We are expecting two additional shipments on Friday—but we will talk more about it in a few minutes. Now, team, Tommy is going to need everyone. You know this is not his first time covering, but I'm asking you to give him your support, if he asks for it. Okay?"

Positive verbal indications of 'yes' came from the team.

"So, we will be back in town early Sunday evening. But we will be available by phone all the time for emergencies." He paused and looked around the room. "That's it! We're done; let's rock this day!"

Today was a really tough day for me at work.

Nurses are, the vast majority of us anyway, *fierce*. We are fiercely protective of our patients, the rights of our patients and our licenses to practice. Most people believe that the physicians are the do all and end all of the patient's care. Not true. A physician can write any order, but the nurse must be smart enough to know whether to carry them out or not. I won't open the nurse/physician debate right now. But some things are true whether we know or believe it or not.

What most people probably really don't know about nurses is that when we lose a patient, we are devastated. It hurts so much. And we cry. We cry hard and continuously. We cry thoroughly as though we hold life and death in our hands. Even though clearly and obviously, we do not.

Today, we lost a patient on the operating room table—not in the usual 'lost a patient on the table' way—but to organ procurement. He was 19 years old, beautiful and healthy. He met with his demise while travelling at a high rate of speed and tricking on his motorcycle. The driver of the vehicle claimed he did not see Johnathan. Others claimed the driver refused to give up the right of way.

Johnathan was brought to the operating room suites in his ICU bed, on a ventilator with his nurse, a respiratory therapist and surrounded by love. His mother and father, two sisters, an aunt, his maternal grandparents and his paternal grandmother were surrounding his bed as he arrived. Holding his hand was a tiny statured female, I would guess not a day over 18, crying with every step. Eyes reddened, somewhat dishevelled and inconsolable.

I met the family at the entrance of the OR suites. This is where they had to say their goodbyes. I waited while one by one the family members touched, kissed and said goodbye.

His girlfriend, I assumed, stood firm in her space, and no one attempted to say goodbye from that side. They understood.

His mother said her tearful goodbye and stepped back after touching the hand of his girlfriend indicating its time.

His mother then came to me, "I need his death to mean something. I want them to take everything that they can. I want them to help as many people as they can. He used to say (mimicking his boyhood voice) 'mommy, I'm going to help people when I grow up! I'm going to be a doctor or a scientist. I'm going to heal people!'" She cried just a little more. "Maybe this is what he meant. Maybe he always knew."

His mother blew her nose, wiped her eyes and with full composure said, "Take care of my baby." She pulled his girlfriend away. "Don't let them take anything above his neck. That's my only request, and I've told everybody. I want him to look like himself." She and the girlfriend embraced, the family formed a circle and we rolled into the OR suite.

I hate organ harvestings. I do. But they are perhaps the most important surgical procedures ever perfected. They are the biggest blessing a person can receive and one that can never be repaid to the giver. I always cry. I get it. I get what we are doing. But I always cry. This is one of the few instances when we bring a patient in and a better life for them is not the primary goal.

A few weeks later, we will get a letter from the consortium telling us of the recipients and the differences our team made in their lives. Sometimes we get letters of thanks from the recipients themselves. Understanding that through the love of these families, who can give the ultimate gift, lives are made better and other people live. I have never seen greater love. That gets me through until the next time.

Thank God, because there is not enough black raspberry ice cream in the world to comfort me through this.

Chapter 7

Greta held Cameron's hand as he drove the two of them home after work. They seemed to finally be getting beyond whatever happened all those weeks ago. In fact, they seemed to be closer than ever. Cameron was far more attentive and sincerely committed to their lives together as husband and wife, and so was she. Greta felt completely loved.

Smiling broadly, Greta blurted, "Niagara Falls, huh?"

Smiling just as broad, Cameron nodded and said, "Niagara Falls." He raised her hand and kissed it. "You said you've always wanted to go. What I didn't tell you is we're going to need our passports because we're going to the Canadian side as well!" He laughed.

"Are you kidding me? Cam! But in three days?"

"We can do it!"

"Wow, you're just full of surprises, aren't you? And I didn't expect you to announce our engagement to the team!"

"I don't know," he said, "but I feel like telling the world!"

"Cam, you said something else in the meeting and you've said it before—talking about not being a perfect man." Shaking her head, Greta said, "You don't have to say that. I know you completely. And I love you. You are perfect for me in every way. I don't care about any of your past. I love you for our future, despite your past. I will never want more than you. I need you to know that. Perfect people don't exist. But sometimes, you luck out and find someone who is *im*perfect for you, just as you are."

"What are you trying to do, make me cry or something!" He laughed. "Wow! I liked that." Cameron leant and initiated a quick lip kiss.

"I don't know though. Seems like our love might make some people sick!"

"What do you mean?" Cameron inquired.

"You saw Lisa! She ran out, saying she was about to vomit, and it wasn't a joke!"

"Yeah, I saw that. But it didn't have anything to do with us," Cameron responded more on the serious side.

Tapping Cam's hand, Greta said, "I'm only kidding, silly! I didn't really think that it did." Greta laughed it off.

Cameron laughed too. "I know! I know! I was only kidding too!" Cameron changed the subject, "So where are we on colour schemes and planning? You really haven't said anything but 'yes' so far."

"I've been thinking, and I'm not sure yet. I want to pick a few then bring it to you and we decide together," Greta answered. "The girls and I are having a sleepover. It was going to be this weekend, but we changed it to next weekend. I love you—because of our Niagara Falls trip." She paused then asked, "Have you thought about what you want?"

"Yes, I have," he readily answered, no thought needed. "I want to get married soon. I don't want to wait six months or a year. I want to do it as soon as we can reasonably pull it together. I'm ready for us to set the date now. I don't have the date, but I know I want it before the end of summer."

"Really?" a bit surprised, Greta added, "Okay. I'm okay with that. We can do that."

The weekend in Niagara Falls came and passed, and the girls were at Greta's surrounded by several tablets, phones and a thousand bridal magazines. The three Gs were joined by Stassi, Greta's soon to be sister-in-law, who was one of her bridesmaids and closer to Cameron than any person in his family. Stassi, being at their wedding, was as important to Greta as the Gs. She knew everything that Stassi had done to get them to this point. Without her, they would not have made the first six months.

We'd looked at a lot of dresses and so far, she did not "see it yet." So, drinking wine, laughing and eating pizza had been our biggest accomplishment over the past one and a half hours.

Then Greta spurted out, "I know I want coral," looking up from Pinterest, "Google colours that go well with coral. I am stuck between, coral and ivory; coral and gold; or coral, black and white. Do you see it?"

"I see it, I like the coral and navy. What about coral and navy?" I asked.

Stassi interrupted, holding an open bridal magazine to her chest, "It may depend on the venue. Have you thought about, indoors, outdoors, destination, afternoon, evening?"

"I want," Greta said in a somewhat daydreaming state of responding, "an outdoor, beautiful green grass with a varying shade of pink floral paths with beautiful green trees in the background…"

"You want the Botanical Gardens or the Arboretum!" Stassi said excitedly.

"YES! Exactly!" Greta exclaimed. "Oh my God, we have to see which one is available! Cameron wanted to do this by the end of the summer. That barely gave us just over two months."

"Why so soon, Greta?" asked Gabby. "What's the rush?" She reached for the wine bottle and refilled her glass. She offered me more, but I covered my glass with my hand, shaking my head "no". It's a sleepover, but I must pace myself with these girls who really knocked them back. But I noticed just at that moment that Greta had not been drinking; her first wine glass was still full.

"Greta," I asked, "are you drinking or not? This isn't a 'let's hurry up and get married before the baby comes' wedding, is it?"

"No, silly!" She laughed. "We're just ready!"

We heard keys unlocking the door, and very soon thereafter Cameron appeared. He came and sat on the arm of the chair where Greta was sitting and gave her a quick kiss.

"I've got colours for you to look at," Greta said, "What do you think?"

Cameron looked, but easily knew what he liked. "I like this with the different shades of pink, with the coral and black. It will make us all look good. The coral and black combination is perfect for the guys. By the way, I'm not getting married in white! Don't even think about it!"

"Wow," Gabby said, "He really knows what he wants and doesn't want!"

We laughed.

"What do you think about the Arboretum or Botanical Gardens?" Greta asked.

"I love it," he answered with feelings and repeated, "I love it. But our timing may not be good. Can we get either of them?"

"We are going to check tomorrow," she said.

Cameron kissed Greta again, then got up to head out. He stopped by his sister, put his hand on top of her head and scrubbed her hair around, messing it up a bit. "Hello squirt!"

"Stop!" she quickly admonished him. "And stop calling me that!" (He called her that all her life. He said she squirted out to ruin his life. He now uses it as a term of endearment.) She hit his hand. "If you want to make it to your wedding, you'd better watch it! And Mom said to call her!"

Cameron and Stassi had developed a very close relationship in the past few years. She had been his strongest supporter through his dependency, and most especially when their family were not accepting Gabby, she stood beside him and supported them both. Her support of their relationship without a doubt, swayed her family to become less overtly critical of a potential black Hispanic daughter-in-law. Even when he did not realise he wanted or needed her help, she was there for him.

"I don't know her number," Cameron said, laughing and walking out of the room.

"I'm going to tell her you said you don't want to talk to her," Stassi yelled behind him.

"I'm going to call her!" Cameron yelled back.

We talked until one by one each person started to retreat to their sleeping areas. I was sleeping on the sofa, and the last one left with Greta. She brought my linen, sat and said, "No, I'm not pregnant. But I stopped taking my birth control months before the race. I'm trying to prepare my body. I want to give him a child as soon as possible."

I could see the concern running through her mind. "What if I can't get pregnant? What if I can't give him the thing he wants most of all?" She shook her head.

"Greta, you are so getting ahead of yourself."

"Maybe I am. But I am scared for some reason."

"That's perfectly normal, Greta," I said. "And it's okay. Everything is going to be fine. Now it may take some time for your body to get back to its baseline from the birth control before you get pregnant, but don't start worrying about it now!"

"I know," she lamented. "But I can't really help it. You don't get how important having a child is to him."

"First thing," I said, "there are many options if you have problems conceiving. But most importantly, what you're doing to yourself right now, is so counterproductive! But I get it. I also know it will be alright. It's way too early to be worried about that right now!"

"I know..." she said quietly.

I reached over and gave her a hug, saying, "That's why you should still be drinking!"

"Oh, you got jokes, huh?"

Chapter 8

Oliver had been working at the Kitchen for over two months now. He and Gabby had developed kind of a weird friendship, a closeness and support system that dared not go too far. He was careful not to say too much, and she was careful not to overreact. They liked and respected each other.

Oliver found Gabby doing inventory in the dry pantry when he arrived. "What are you doing?" he asked puzzled because he had long since been doing inventory.

"Good morning, Oliver, and inventory," she answered simply.

"Yeah, I see that. But why? I can do that," he explained.

Stopping and turning to look at him for the first time since his arrival, Gabby noticed that he had cut his hair to a couple of inches above his shoulders and perhaps even had gotten highlights. He had new clothes and appeared renewed. His light blue pullover snugly fit his chest and arms then disappeared into the relaxed black jeans on his slim and overtly sexy 6'1" body.

"Wow! Look at you! You look great! Who are you trying to woo?" Gabby laughed.

"No one," he said, attempting to take the tablet Gabby was entering the numbers into.

Gabby quickly pulled the tablet away, denying him access. "Oh, you're trying to get somebody's attention!" She laughed.

"Gabby, is it possible that I'm just making some simple changes for myself? Can that, at least, be a possibility?" They were both laughing. Then he said, "Gabby! Why. Are. You. Doing. Inventory? Did I screw it up last month?"

Gabby stopped and seriously gave her full attention to Oliver. Then answered him.

"You did it very well last month, Oliver. Just like everything else you do around here. I have come to depend upon you in so many ways in a really short period of time." She sighed in appreciation. "So, I want to do something for you. I'm trying to get things caught up, so I can give you a few days off."

Oliver turned a wooden crate on its side and sat on it. He shook his head. "You have no idea how much that means to me." He thought on that for a few seconds before continuing. "But, I don't need any time off."

"I didn't say you needed time off. I said I want to give you some time off. I want to give you a break."

"But I don't want a break."

"Oliver, why is nothing simple with you?"

"I'm not a simple man!" He laughed.

"You can say that again! Let me do something for you," Gabby almost pleaded. "You work six out of seven days, sometimes seven of seven. You streamlined our processes and made changes that have drastically improved everything we do here. I just want to show my appreciation. I want to do something for you."

"You already have. I really don't want any time off," he said.

"Two days?" Gabby asked.

"How about, you owe me one?" Oliver compromised. "When I need the time, I will let you know and you will have no choice but to say yes." He stood, walked to her and extended his hand to shake on it.

They shook hands as she reluctantly said, "Okay. But I can't believe that you don't have something that you want to do!"

"I do," he said, looking directly into her eyes. "But the timing's not right yet. However, I'm hopeful! So, what's up with you?"

Gabby placed the tablet in Oliver's hands. "I'm going to tell you this, and don't judge me!"

"I'm in no position to judge anybody," he said. "Tell me."

"I've been talking to Calvin every day for the past couple of weeks."

"Have you been hanging out with him?" Oliver asked, looking away from her and starting the inventory.

"No. We just talk for hours on the phone, right now. But I can see that changing."

"Congratulations," Oliver still did not look at her and had no enthusiasm in his voice.

"What does that mean?"

"It means 'congratulations'."

"He's not so bad, Oliver," Gabby said.

"You don't have to convince me, Gabby. I can hear wedding bells."

"You know, Oliver…never mind." She left the pantry.

I was on my way back to China Express. I ordered Shrimp and Broccoli, and when I got home, I found out that I had Chicken and Broccoli. This was the second time this had happened from this restaurant. But it's the closest one to me and I could easily pick up dinner on my way home from work. Now I was paranoid. Many years ago, it was truthfully reported on the news (not fake news!) that a certain Chinese restaurant was using meat from animals other than chicken, pork, beef or seafood and closed by the Department of Health. Animals of a domestic and other nature. We had been ordering take out for lunch at work from there for years.

The story literally made me sick. However, I really do love the convenience and taste of Chinese food. And I absolutely do not believe all Chinese Food restaurants use domestic and other animals typically not ingested in the United States. But I cannot trust that alone. My remedy, I only eat shrimp. Something I am certain to recognise. It costs a little more, but I'm okay with that.

The first time this happened, I was home in my PJs, in front of the TV and comfortable, so it wasn't worth it to go back out. I didn't eat it. But I didn't return it. Today, however, I'd done none of that. I was taking it back.

Now you know it can't be that simple. As I was driving back, I was bombarded with thoughts of how to handle this. My biggest fear was getting beaten down by three Chinese guys over some shrimp and broccoli, someone videoing the incident, putting it on YouTube and the video going viral. You see, I knew they were going to want to give me my original order, just correct it. But I was paranoid about restaurants. I never sent anything back and I never gave anybody a chance to re-make anything for me. I was afraid they would do bad things to my food. I just wanted my money back. My dilemma was how do I get my money back without any drama.

I remembered mall shopping once, and I went by the food court where some woman was berating the staff at a certain very common fast food restaurant because they got her order wrong. It was quite a spectacle and it really upset me to see how she disrespected them. Though she was talking to the cashier initially, what she was saying was disrespectful to all of the employees. You could see on their faces how they were feeling. She said things like "You're stupid as f…, that's why you're working here. You're too f…ing ignorant to get a job anywhere else. Get me the f…ing manager if you know how to do that!" The cashier got the manager who was attempting to defuse the situation, so the customer cussed her out too. So, she got her order and left rudely. I saw her as I was leaving about five minutes later. She was heading back in the direction of the well-known fast food restaurant. She apparently remembered me from the initial incident and said, "I'm going right back, they still didn't get it right!"

My initial inclination was to tell her, "Lady, just take the L". But of course, I did not. If she was crazy enough to go back asking for more food, that she planned to ingest or give to her family—after the way she had treated the staff, well, she deserved all the DNA and floor dirt and slime she was going to get. I imagined everyone took turns spitting or doing whatever to the missing item she went back for. Not that I knew that happened—but that was my greatest fear about upsetting people who were preparing my food. Besides, we've all seen the horrendous viral videos. Now maybe she deserved it. Some people are so disrespectful to others. And some people are exceedingly vindictive. People get sensitive and ruin your food in the worst way.

At any rate, as I was driving back, I was considering what to do. My decision, first and foremost, was to approach them very quietly, not to bring the drama. When they offer to remake the order, I would ask quietly, "Is it possible for me to just get my money back?" And lastly, if they do not want to return my money, I would just leave the wrong order and take the L.

I walked in and there's a full row of people waiting on the carry-out wall as well as one or two dine-in clients. I got in line with my bag in my hand. I recognised the guy who took my order, and I could see the other two in the back. I asked the cashier if he remembered me. He looked at me as though he had no idea, and I flashed the receipt. He did not acknowledge anything but looked at me like, "What's the deal?" I told about the order mix-up. He said he could redo my order. Darn it.

I asked for my money back very quietly. No one had heard any of our interaction. I was very calm and quiet through all. He gave me my money back.

Okay! So, it was anti-climactic! But I was really troubled for a while!

Gabby had decided that she was going to allow Calvin to come over and, more than likely, spend the night. She wanted that intimacy. She decided he was the one to break the drought. He had shown a sustained interest in her. For months! Surely, he had a greater interest than a one-night stand. Surely, he saw something deeper. During their lengthy conversations, he assured her that he had no interest in anyone else but made it clear that he wanted to bed her. That was not a turn-off. In fact, feeling wanted was something she really appreciated.

But somehow Oliver was in her head. His judgmental attitude was standing next to her while she dressed and put on make-up, waiting for Calvin to arrive. She shook it off.

"I'm not going to let Oliver ruin my night. I am so ready right now. Besides, it doesn't have to last forever, just through this night. Then I will think about it later."

She was cooking dinner; Calvin had been asking her to cook for him for weeks. You can't go wrong with basic salmon, rice and asparagus. She had run by The Cheesecake Factory and picked up a lemon-raspberry cheesecake for dessert. When the doorbell rang, everything that she wanted in place, was in place. She was ready to have a wonderful evening of good company, conversation, and dinner followed by a passionate session of lovemaking.

But she was not ready for the hot and heavy kiss Calvin pressed upon her when she opened the door. He was like some manner of a sexual beast with a single vision, to ravish her. She wanted to be ravished, but not exactly this way.

"I want to make love to you right now," Calvin said through heavy breathing, kisses and caressing her body.

Gabby was ambivalent, but she was so hot, so ready. She scrapped the other planned evening agenda, and they headed to the bedroom.

There was no foreplay or intimacy associated with their first act. She came. He came. Then immediately thereafter, while he was still inside of her, he started snoring. He felt so heavy on top of her. She nudged him, and he seemed to just nestle himself in deeper and more snugly.

"Damnit," she said, looking around, contemplating her next move.

After about 15 minutes of hardcore sleeping or power napping—his body quickly jerked. He woke and looked at her, gave her a quick kiss and said, "I've got to go. I promised my mom I would come to help her with some things tonight." He jumped up with a clear purpose to leave immediately and began dressing.

Gabby was almost shocked. She said nothing, just watched and listened.

"You cooked, right?" he asked, "How about fixing me a plate to take with me?"

"Why not?" she responded and grabbed her robe and left the room.

She gave him the old, should have already been tossed out, spaghetti stained, fake tupperware.

Chapter 9

The three Gs and Stassi met to search for wedding venues. As luck would have it, the Botanical Gardens had, moments earlier, got a cancellation for the last Saturday before fall. They secured the venue. Stassi had to leave but the three Gs went to lunch. Gabby began to share. "I let Calvin come over last night," she said.

"And...?" We beckoned to her for details.

"I'm not sure it's the smartest thing I've done in my life..." she said.

"Why?" I asked, "what happened or didn't happen?"

"Well, it was..." she stopped and gave thought to her description of what happened. "It was like a targeted sex session. No feeling, just sex. I don't know; I had visualised it being very different."

"Does that mean you didn't enjoy it?" Greta asked.

"Well, no. I came!" she said and laughed a little. "My God, that thing was big!! Just saying, it was BIG!!! But..." she quickly came back to her initial concerns, "no condom."

"Are you kidding me," I was surprised. Gabby was not into sex. She had, according to her, not been with a man since Travis died eight years ago and no other man prior to Travis. Not only did she, but no condom? Yikes! "So why are you feeling so whatever about it?"

"That Oliver!" she quickly spouted out. "Looks like he might be right. Calvin couldn't get out of there quick enough. I almost felt used."

"I think Oliver likes you for himself," Greta said.

"I do too," I added.

"He doesn't like me romantically—" Gabby started.

I interrupted, "I think you're wrong. I think he does. I've seen you two around each other. There is something there."

"No, he's told me. He thinks I'm special for what I bring to the world. Helping people, you know."

"How blind are you?" I asked almost in disbelief. "Do you know how many of us would love to have someone who thinks we make a difference in the WORLD? The world, Gabby! You're stupid," I said, shaking my head.

"You didn't hear the conversation, Giselle. Anyway, you're always saying how you don't want or need a relationship. But sounds like you are saying something different now."

I quickly changed the subject, "Greta, I can't believe you got the Botanical Gardens!"

"I know, right!" she said quickly, "But are you saying you want someone to think you make a difference in the world?"

"Both of you are stupid!"

"When's the last time you had some?" Greta continued, "Maybe you are finally ready for some, some – you know!"

"You know," Gabby interjected, "you cannot go indefinitely without sex!"

"How did this turn into a conversation about me? I'm good!" I said, thinking about the Light bulb man AKA Kevin Harper, Deputy Fire Chief. But I certainly didn't tell these two hounds about him. I would never live it down!

Greta was excited to let Cameron know that she had found and secured the venue they both wanted. She reached for the doorknob to his office and it opened from the inside before she could touch it. Coming out and clearly emotional was Lisa, the waitress who got nauseated during the team meeting.

"Are you okay?" Greta asked, quite concerned.

"Sure," Lisa responded quietly and walked away quickly.

Greta felt relatively certain she knew what the problem was. She went into the office, and Cameron was obviously affected as well. They embraced lovingly, kissed and then embraced a little longer.

"Hi, baby," Greta said. "Good news. We've got our venue! We got the Botanical Gardens and on the last weekend of summer!"

A feeling of relief came over him. "Fantastic! I love you so much! I can't wait to make you my wife. It's like, I don't know what I was waiting for." He kissed her again. "I have a thought, what if we have a ceremony right now at a Justice of the Peace, but still have a beautiful wedding at the end of the summer? Let's get married now. Today!"

Greta pulled back. "Cameron, why? What's up with you?"

"I think it was from talking to Lisa—" he began.

Greta interrupted both inquisitively and knowingly, "She's pregnant, isn't she!"

"Yes," he answered. "By someone who does not love her and never will. It was a mistake, and he's not interested in ruining his life for her."

"That's kind of hard. Men can be such jerks sometimes! They both made the mistake! So, what is she going to do?"

Cameron said, initially sitting on his desk while he and Greta kissed, rose, went around the desk and sat in his chair, "I don't know. I think she's trying to figure it out. She just wanted me to know what was going on with her. You know in case it affected her job performance."

"Makes sense. I'm sorry for her," Greta said, "Cameron, do you really want to get married first?" sitting on the desk near him. "Because I will if that's what you need. But don't do it because you see the problems that other people are having. I love you. We're already on for life!"

"No," he resolved. "We can wait. I guess now that I know that I want to do it, it's hard to wait."

"I love you," Greta said. "I will see you tonight. We have an appointment in an hour at the Bridal Shoppe."

It had been over a week had since Gabby's tryst with Calvin. They had talked a few times but not every day and far less in length. But it really didn't bother her so much. She felt herself being less accommodating toward him more than the opposite. She intentionally did not answer his calls from time to time. Something had happened. She knew his interests were not the same as hers, and she was cutting her losses.

But she had not shared any of it with Oliver. She wasn't sure if she would or not. They continued to work well together if relationships were not discussed. So maybe it's better to not share that with him. Greta was at the reception counter, and a young, clearly not homeless white female came in.

"Hi. Is Oliver available?" she inquired.

"He is," For some odd reason, Gabby was taken aback. "May I tell him who's asking for him?"

"Lynne," she answered with a beautiful smile, showcasing a mouth full of glistening white, perfect teeth.

"Have a seat. I'll get him."

Gabby went to the back, and Oliver was updating the weekly volunteer assignment board. She walked up and stood next to him, paused for a moment, then said, "Lynne is here. She's waiting for you out front."

Oliver looked at her as though he was gauging her response to the fact that Lynne had come and the potential implications. "Thanks." He took off his apron, washed his hands and walked out front, leaving Gabby in the prep area.

After talking to Lynne, Oliver knocked on Gabby's office door which was half-open.

"Hey," he said, not completely entering the office, "you remember that promise for a day off? How's this weekend? Saturday and Sunday?"

"Sure," Gabby said quickly, her voice almost cracking. She was attempting to hide that she felt a sense of loss, even hurt that he was asking for time off to spend with someone. She did not want to know with any degree of certainty who this girl was. The implications were almost more than she wanted to consider. "Enjoy yourself," she said with a very well-acted, though forced, smile.

I had another tough day at work. The vast majority of the patients we take to surgery require reassurance and support that is easy to provide—this is what we do. But every now and then, there is no reassurance to be given. Case in point—a young couple whose 12-week foetus succumbed in utero but did not expel and we had to evacuate the products of conception. Young couple, first child. Both devastated. There were no words to comfort them. I went in and sat with them. I didn't offer the typical things people say. I've done enough of these to know, that the "You're young. You can try again" speech does not help in any way at the loss of a child. I gave her the box of tissues after giving him a couple first. I sat quietly with them a few moments, in solidarity of their loss. Before leaving, I said, "Please let me know if there's anything that I can do, I'm Giselle—anyone can get me for you."

I find that I feel the pain, regardless of origin when interacting with my patients. Maybe I'm like that Star Trek Empath—but I really love people and care about what they are going through, regardless of who they are. I cannot stand to see others suffer, abused or in need. Being a nurse has given me a lifelong opportunity to be compassionate and help others. But after so many years, it's taking its toll on me. I think of my patients after I leave the job. I pray for them before I even meet them and then again after I meet them.

As I was entering my building, I was wondering if the young couple was okay and wondering about saying another prayer for them. Going into the building about 20 feet ahead of me, I saw a man carrying his cleaned laundry over his shoulder. Once I got inside the building and to the elevator, he was still standing there. The elevator arrived just as I did, and I followed him onto it. I hit my button and backed up against the wall, checking my text messages without even looking at him.

"Hi," he said.

I looked up and I felt myself literally jumping out of my body! Yes, somehow it was him—the light bulb man—AKA Kevin Harper, Deputy Fire Chief. Only he and I were on the elevator. Together. Alone. In my building!

I managed to squeak out a "Hello".

"I know you," he said.

"You do?" Okay, I thought to myself, this is interesting... and crazy!

"Well, I don't *know* you," he said. "But you were one of the first people I saw when I moved in here, and I saw you a couple of times after, at Lowe's. I went in for light bulbs, and you were buying some too. I'm Kevin."

"I'm Giselle." All the time I was thinking, I remember you—but I did not say that though. "So, you're new to this building?"

"Yes, but I'm a firefighter, so I'm not here all the time. You probably haven't seen me here before. But I've seen you several times."

"Oh, okay," I said.

The elevator door opened, and I noticed we both were on the 5th floor.

"Nice to finally meet you, *Giselle,*" he said as he was heading in the opposite direction.

The fact that he said 'nice to finally meet you' was not wasted on me at all. But I just said, "Nice to meet you, Kevin." And left it at that.

I had literally been fighting with myself not to think about this man. And he lived in my building! I was completely thrown at that moment. Plus, he had seen me before I became obsessed with him as the semi-rude light bulb man! What was happening here?

Alright, girl! Get a hold of yourself. Calm down. Come back to reality. Let it go. Do whatever you need to do. But don't get caught up, don't fall...

Chapter 10

Monday morning. Gabby was in for some sort of a strange day. Calvin was making a delivery this morning, and Oliver was back from his weekend with the beautifully teethed, Miss Lynne. One thing Gabby was sure of, she did not want to see Calvin at all. She decided to leave a note for Oliver that she was not to be disturbed or interrupted for any reason this morning and for him to receive the delivery without her. That would take care of Calvin. But she had to figure out what would happen with Oliver. Their relationship was odd, and as she had just learned, on both sides.

Calvin attempted to call her three times this morning and left messages for her to call him. She had elected not to. His intention was to talk to her at the Kitchen but was met by Oliver alone.

"Gabrielle around?" he inquired, looking around.

"She's not available today," Oliver responded.

"When will she be available?" Calvin persisted.

"I don't know the answer to that."

Calvin began to feel upset and ignored. "You don't like me, do you?"

Oliver, without emotions, signed the delivery, completed the transaction and turned his attention away. "I don't feel anything about you. But I will tell Gabby you were very interested in seeing her."

Calvin was angered by what he thought was disrespectful and attempted to get some eye contact, but Oliver never looked at him.

"Man. I'm not going to let you upset me this early in the morning. You don't even matter." Calvin abruptly left after those words. Oliver continued with his daily tasks.

After the delivery, Oliver chose not to seek Gabby out. He figured she would be out soon enough. They could talk then.

Lisa had become more a difficult to manage employee as she moved further along in her pregnancy. She had been calling out and coming in late, even on their busiest days. Cameron typically did not tolerate this from the employees because of the effect on the restaurant, staff morale and the customers. Today, Lisa was late again. Greta attempted to have a conversation with her, but Lisa shut her down quickly.

"I can't talk about this right now. Yes, I'm late, so maybe you need to let me get started instead of holding me up to talk!" Lisa walked away, leaving Greta perplexed.

Greta decided it was best to get through dinner service and speak with Cameron at home to make some decisions on moving forward with Lisa. Greta recognised that there were strong life-changing issues that Lisa was dealing with. But her behaviour was unacceptable and set a detrimental precedence.

That night, both Greta and Cameron were tired; there had been a higher than normal volume for dinner service on a Monday—in fact, it seemed more like a Friday. It was late, and they got into a hot shower together. Their attraction was very strong. It seemed to grow more and more as time progressed. They made shower love—always good.

While drying off, Greta remembered the issue with Lisa and decided to bring it up.

"I've been meaning to talk to you about Lisa," she said. "You know, usually you are on top of these things. I know you've been feeling sorry for her. But she's getting out of hand. We need to do something. She went off on me today, and she actually has been really slow to interact with me for a few weeks now."

"I know." He shook his head. "Let's talk about it in a minute."

They both put on their comfy night clothes. Greta climbed into bed but Cameron did not. He sat in the huge aqua plush chair (that was perfectly coordinated with their aqua, brown and white bedroom colour scheme) near the bedroom window. Greta grabbed her cell phone to check messages and, of course, Facebook.

Cameron sat, alternating between looking at her and dropping his face into his hands. He finally built up enough courage and just said it, "Lisa's baby may be mine." Greta looked up, eyebrows nearly on the roof.

"I'm sorry, what?" She could not have just heard what she thought she heard.

Cameron took a deep breath. "Lisa says I am the father of her baby."

Greta dropped her phone on the bed, sat up totally erect and looked at him, attempting to grasp something she was having a lot of difficulty hearing and understanding. She was still and quiet.

She managed a shocked response, "But how can that be possible, Cam?"

Cameron explained, "After we argued the day of the race, I went to work. Like I said, I was really thinking about taking a drink. Lisa was there; she was the opener, and we started to talk. I don't really know how it happened, but we ended up having sex. I regretted it immediately. I wanted to tell you. I even tried to tell you what I had done—but I couldn't. Then a couple of days before the staff meeting, she told me she was pregnant, and that I was the father." He waited for a reaction. "I don't know what to do right now. I can't lose you. I can't…" he said near tears.

"Wait," she said to bring a halt to everything he was saying. "Wait. Wait. Wait. Wait. Just fricking wait! Don't talk. Don't say another word. Don't say another word."

Greta got out of bed and walked, dazed and confused, into their bathroom. She washed her face with cold water and emerged about five minutes later, seeing that Cameron was still sitting in the same place. She walked over to him, and with all the power in her, she slapped what she hoped would be, the full-blown shit out of him.

Cameron took the slap with little reaction and no return.

Greta furiously shouted, "I can't believe you! I can't believe you! How could you?"

She walked to the window and placed her hands over her face. She could not control the tears. "You're forcing me to make a decision to live without you when that's the absolute last thing on this earth I want to do!"

"I'm not a perfect man, Greta. But I love you. And I love only *you*," he stated quietly.

"Oh. Right!" she said, wiping her eyes with her bare hands, "You're not a perfect man." She sarcastically added, "You are not a perfect man! Well, that makes it all right then, doesn't it? You're not a perfect man! But you certainly are a jackass!"

"No, it does not. I know that," he said.

"You can get some random girl pregnant, and it's okay because you are not a perfect man! You can ruin both of our lives because you are not a perfect man! Well, guess what, buster? I'm not a perfect woman either, but I have never, ever been unfaithful to you! And just so you know, I've had more than my share of opportunities!" she confessed.

"I'm sure you've had many opportunities to be unfaithful, Greta. I'm sure of that." He paused and took a breath. "I only love you. I made a mistake. But I only love and want to be with you."

"Did you know she was pregnant when you proposed?"

"No. I only knew that by having sex with her, I had made the biggest mistake of my life. Even if she wasn't pregnant, I knew I had betrayed you. I knew you deserved better. The guilt was killing me. I wanted to tell you. To be completely honest, the day I proposed, I didn't know if I was going to propose or break up. I was trying to tell you what happened with Lisa and let you break up with me if you wanted to. And propose if I could. But as I tried," he paused and thought. "When you cried…" he paused again. "I love you." He teared up again. "I love only you."

"Oh my God. Oh my God. Oh my God!" Greta started to sob loudly with her face in her hands. "I can't believe I didn't see this coming! Right under my nose!"

Cameron came to her and attempted to console her.

Greta used both fists and hit him repeatedly in his chest, though without the force of the slap. "Don't! Just get away from me, you jackass! Just get away from me!"

"I'm sorry."

"You're not sorry! Or you wouldn't have done it in the first place!"

"It wasn't planned. We were not having some sordid affair. It only happened once. I know that doesn't matter right now. But I love you. I love you," he said with his hands on her shoulders as though he could shake that truth into her and make it matter, "and I love only you. I made a mistake. I know that. But I think it would be a much bigger mistake if we let us go because of it." He let go as she squirmed for his release.

Cameron left the room in sadness and slept on the sofa.

Greta had decided to keep Cameron's infidelity to herself, at least for now. They were sleeping in separate rooms but were still under the same roof. She knew that he loved her. She knew that he had made a mistake. But was the cost of that mistake hers to pay. Because she loved him too. So, she waited, staying, trying to figure it all out. They were less than four weeks out from the wedding now. Invitations had been sent; the venue secured. And while they were not sleeping together or even talking as much, their connection seemed stronger than ever. She actually still *felt* loved by him.

One big problem for Greta was that she had been trying to get pregnant and give Cameron his first child in the same time frame that Lisa had actually got pregnant. She was sick about all of this. But she desperately loved the man. Did it make her weak to stay and support him through whatever?

This morning, thinking about it made her stomach queasy. And she didn't want to see his face. He was waiting for her downstairs to go to work together, and she texted him to go ahead without her. She had a lot of difficulties believing that he had put her in this position. She was so angry with him. And still did not want to let him go.

After Cameron had gone, she went downstairs, put a green tea/chamomile mint in the Keurig and decided to just sit for a minute. The first sip—and she had to run to the bathroom. To throw up. "Am I pregnant?" she asked herself.

She bought a random over the counter pregnancy test and the results were *positive.* So, the plot thickened.

"I can't tell him." She needed her girls. She texted Cameron that she would not be in and called me and Gabby to see if we could meet up.

I had a rare off day, and Gabby was glad to leave The Kitchen for a few hours. We agreed to meet at Greta's.

Greta decided to not hold back. Once we were all there, she came straight to the point.

"Cameron got a waitress at work pregnant," she said.

Gasps from both of us. "Are you kidding?" I asked in total shock.

Greta started crying. We moved close to her one on each side and tried to console her. But we were also somewhat in disbelief. We liked Cameron and everything that he appeared to represent as a man in a relationship.

Just wow.

"Men are such jerks!" Gabby blurted, "Sometimes, I wish I liked vagina, so I wouldn't have to deal with them at all!"

"Well, some vaginas are jerks too, I'm sure!" I suggested. "It's all about the person."

So, we're trying to get through this bombshell, then Greta dropped the biggest one of all.

"I'm pregnant too!" she said, crying even more.

Gabby leant away from her and almost instantaneously said, "Daaayyyuumm!"

We all paused for a moment to absorb what was just said.

"Okay. It's okay," I said, "It's okay," trying to calm us all down. "Any plans?"

"I just found out two hours ago," she whimpered. "I feel like I need Bridget's wisdom. What would she say?"

"She would definitely say keep it, *only if you are going to love it and treat it right. It's not the child's fault what the parents are or what they do,*" I said.

"Yes," Gabby added, "that's exactly what she said to her niece. She loved children and often said that children don't stand a chance against the adults in this world. She said everything always came down to parenting. It's all about the love of the parents—or lack thereof."

"She was not a proponent of abortion; she was a proponent of the child and its best interests once it got here," I added.

"I'm not getting an abortion," Greta said, "I don't know what to do about all of this. It's like, too much!" crying even more, "And I can't tell Cameron about the baby yet. The wedding day is almost here. I just don't know."

Soon we were all crying. We did not help her in the least.

But every time I came close to wanting a relationship, relationship people helped me quickly figure out why I did not want one!

Chapter 11

I got home and found a note under my door. I opened it to find an invitation to dinner from Kevin, you know, Harper, Deputy Fire Chief AKA the light bulb man. It's for tonight and included his number and was signed by Kevin.

After all the drama with Greta, my mind was mushy and I probably won't be good company. But of course, I called him up and accepted. He invited me to walk with him to a little Italian bistro up the street, and I loved the idea. He said he would come by at 7:00, which only gave me a couple of hours. I could do that though. I liked this guy. But I already knew I didn't want to. I felt that I was a real danger for falling, and I just didn't need that in my life at the moment.

I choose to dress down. Comfy black sweats, a black tank top and red flip flops.

He was perfectly on time. Every time I saw this guy, my heart moved differently from the norm. I didn't invite him in. I was ready, and we just headed out.

The bistro was about three city blocks away. We had a flow to the conversation that just felt good. I started by confessing that I saw him on TV doing an interview.

"I'm required to do those from time to time," he said. "I actually love being a firefighter. It's certainly not your safest job, but it is very important."

"How long have you been a firefighter?" I asked.

"Nearly 25 years now," he said. "I was actually a factory worker before this."

"Really?" I don't know why I was surprised. "Would not have thought that."

"Why?"

"I don't know," I said. "You don't really look like a random factory worker at all. Not that it's a bad career, but to me, you look more like, yeah, a firefighter," I said with a smile.

"I found my thing and stuck with it," he said.

As we arrived at the bistro, he opened the door with his right hand, put his left hand on my lower back and guided me in first. (I liked that!) We were seated. I already knew I wanted the shrimp scampi. I'd had it before, and I tend to stick with what I know I like. He ordered the same thing.

If I'm going to drink, with dinner I usually have a Riesling. I don't really like wine at all, but this is sweet and tends to go well with the scampi—to me.

"So, tell me about yourself," he said.

"Well, I am never too comfortable talking about myself!" I said; I am a bit coy in nature.

"Why not?" he quickly asked.

"I don't know. I never really think about myself, I guess," I said. "But I'm a nurse. I've been a nurse longer than you've been a firefighter; believe it or not. My original plan in college was to major in Broadcast Journalism. My good friend was majoring in nursing and convinced me to change. And the rest is history."

"I can see you as a television reporter," he said, realising that it could have been a good fit. "You certainly have the look, and you're articulate."

"I know right! I say from time to time that I could have been the next Oprah!" We laughed. "But I like being and doing me as I am right now."

I took a bite of the scampi and a sip of wine.

"Okay, your turn. Tell me something about yourself that you want me to know," I said, searching a bit.

"I'm in the middle of a divorce, and my final date is coming very soon. I have been separated for nearly a year now. I will never go back. Because I'm done."

"Oh!" I guess I got what I was searching for! "You want to talk about that, right off the bat, huh?"

"I have nothing to hide."

"You seem a little bit bitter, Kevin, if I can say that to you," I eased my opinion in.

"I hear you. But I'm not bitter; I'm just done," he said. "And before you jump to that conclusion, no. She did not sleep with my best friend or cheat on me. She was not a drug addict or alcoholic or killing me with debt. She just got on my nerves and complained and accused me of things; super jealous; I just could not take it anymore. She liked drama to the millionth power and loved provoking me. So, I left."

Flashback to memories of Harry.

"Kevin," I said, slow-talking him a bit, "are you telling me you are an *asshole*?"

"You tell me. If you know that as a fireman, I must stay at the station a certain number of days and nights during the month, why would that be a problem? Why would my peers know how insecure my wife is, all the while also knowing that I am faithful? It just got to be too much."

"And you just walked away?"

"I didn't *just* walk away!" Kevin said, defending himself. "I can never really explain to you the level of crazy this woman is."

"Kevin, there had to be something about her in the first place that attracted you to her. I mean, you married her for heaven's sake!"

"Oh, so you want to make this hard, huh?" He laughed and shook his head. "I didn't know I was marrying crazy—but there were obviously things about her that I liked, even loved. But not the crazy insecure stuff."

"What did you do to make her feel more secure?" I asked.

"I did try, Giselle. I did," he said convincingly, "but at some point, you get the picture. There's nothing more you can do. So, you cut your losses."

Okay, yes, he *is* an asshole! I thought.

"Wow," I said. I was taken aback. He gave me a clear look at a possible future for us. I could also tell he was beginning to feel flashbacks to the time in the relationship. So, I didn't call him an asshole again, but he was an asshole.

"Listen, I'm too old to spend the rest of my life unhappy and constantly trying to make sure somebody else is happy. I cannot make anyone happy but myself. And the same goes for everyone else." He added, "I remember the first time I saw you (coming back to the here and now). You were getting out of your car to go into our building. I'm sure you had just got off work. I had just worked a three-alarm fire and was sitting in my car. The way you walked, head up, moving with purpose. I said to myself that you had so much confidence, and it was crazy attractive to me. I saw you the next day heading to work. I don't know, it was like, I knew you."

Of course, I was swallowing this BS hook, line and sinker.

"Why didn't you approach me?" I challenged him.

"I did, well, I tried," he quickly corrected himself, "at Lowe's. But when you looked at me, I lost it. And walked away. When I saw you at the cashier, I tried again, but you seemed so disinterested."

I could not help but laugh out loud. "Disinterested, huh?" I kept laughing.

"That's how it seemed to me," he explained. "I had to wait for the right moment. I didn't want to get shut down from the start."

"But, dude, I have to say it, you're an asshole. There was nothing wrong with this woman but insecurity. All you had to do was show her some love, show her that she mattered. But instead, you let her go for a little thing like that!"

"Insecurity is not a little thing, Giselle. I am willing to bet, it ruins more relationships than both money and infidelity," he proclaimed.

"Do you really believe that?" I asked.

"I do. What on earth is attractive about not believing in yourself? You should believe in yourself if nobody else does!"

I listened to him, and all I could think of was 'My God! What kind of life lesson is this!'

As we headed back, his apparently unintentional touching of my hand turned to holding it. I was probably more insecure than he had any idea though. And I run from relationships quickly and often. But for the moment, I liked that.

By the way—the fact that he was trying to talk to me at Lowe's was tucked neatly away in my internal 'YES!' box.

The first face Gabby saw Friday morning when she arrived at The Kitchen was Calvin's—there waiting for her at the entrance. He stopped her.

"I'm not sure why you are ignoring me…" he blurted.

"I'm not ignoring—"

He stopped her mid-sentence, "You can keep all of that! I just want to tell you to see your doctor. I just found out that I have herpes. Sorry." He hastily walked away, leaving Gabby dumbfounded.

At that moment, everything about Gabby's life and her future slowly began to change. She saw the worst-case scenario herpes lesions and never having sex again. Never having a life partner, because she could never disclose this to him. Gabby suddenly felt suicidal.

She went inside, walking almost zombie-like. She had to get a grasp on herself. The first thing was to be sure that she indeed had the disease. That would determine her next course of action. But she was still two hours out before the doctor's office opened. So, she decided to try and behave as though it never happened.

When Oliver arrived, Lynne was with him. He gave her one of his dirty chef's jackets to take to the cleaners for him. He gave her a soft kiss and she left. Gabby was sitting at one of the dining room tables and finally learned that theirs was a romantic relationship. And the vice grip on her heart tightened.

She headed out of the dining room, and Oliver saw her. "Hey, I didn't know you were out here. Good morning," he said.

"Good morning," she said.

"That's got to be the most lacklustre 'good morning' I've ever heard!" he laughed, but she did not respond in kind. She rather headed in the direction of her office.

Oliver followed, "What's wrong?"

"Nothing," she said unconvincingly.

"Gabby, what's wrong?" he asked again.

"Nothing." She couldn't bear to tell him or anyone. "Oliver, can I have a minute?"

Oliver stepped back and let Gabby walk away. He was thinking it was his fault and having to do with Lynne.

Gabby went to Quick Care as soon as it opened. When she called her personal MD, she could not get in for at least a week. She had her labs drawn but turned out she won't get the results for a minimal of 23 days, and if negative, she will need to retest in three to four months, if negative at that time, then perhaps once more at six months to be certain. Unless she developed lesions, at which point, the lesion itself could be swabbed and give her a definitive positive answer. Problem is most people with herpes are asymptomatic, they never have the notorious breakouts or lesions. They can still infect others, but may never know that they have it unless they get a blood test.

Before she could get an answer, she would have to wait the three weeks, at which point they would call her. She was really feeling devastated. She decided that the best thing to do was to go back to work. If she went home, she would only ruminate over the situation.

In her office, she was finding it very difficult to concentrate. She found herself crying somewhat uncontrollably. There was a knock on her door. She had uncharacteristically locked it, giving herself time to pull it together a bit before opening the door.

When she opened the door, Oliver was there with a hot cup of tea for her.

"I brought you some tea. Thought you could use it," he said.

Gabby took the tea, went back to her desk and sat. Her eyes were red and swollen.

"Do you want to talk about it?" Oliver asked, almost begging her to let him in.

Gabby just looked at him and shook her head 'no'. She didn't say a word. She felt tears rising again.

Oliver walked behind her desk and squatted next to her; he turned her toward him and placed his hands on her knees. Very quietly and even heartbroken himself, he asked, "Is it me? Did I do this to you?"

Gabby gave brief thought on whether letting him in was a good idea. And for some reason, she trusted him.

"I had sex with Calvin," she said. "Then I realised he was not someone I wanted to continue a relationship with, and I have been avoiding him since that time. At first, he seemed okay with the dwindling attention, but then he started calling persistently. I just figured he would get the picture and leave me alone. He was here this morning. He was angry. He didn't have much to say." She took a sip of the tea, wiped her nose and continued, "Turns out he wasn't trying to win my affection. He told me he had given me herpes, and that I should go see my doctor."

Though he was quite taken aback, Oliver didn't move his hand from her knees. "I'm so sorry. Did you call your doctor yet?"

"Yes. I couldn't get in today, so I went to Quick Care. I had blood drawn, but it will be more than three weeks before the first results, and I must repeat tests three to four months later to figure out if I'm negative. It takes longer for antibodies to build up for a positive result. It will be six months before I know if I'm in the clear."

"You know, this is not the end of the world. There are medications now…"

"Oliver, how would you feel if you were told you had herpes?"

"That's sort of an unfair question, Gabby," he said.

"Nobody wants to be with the person with herpes."

"Listen," he said, looking up at her, "just wait for the results. You don't know if you actually have a reason for all of this." He raised her head up with her chin and looked directly into her eyes. "I promise you, it will be okay."

"What? No 'I told you so'?" she asked.

"I didn't tell you this. I wish I could have, though. I would have protected you." He rose and wiped her tears using the thumbs of both hands simultaneously. He kissed her on the forehead and whispered, "Feel better; it will be okay."

She did feel better. And she believed it would be okay. But she cried more.

Chapter 12

The girls were here hanging out at my place tonight. We were going to watch some YouTube comedians and hopefully get our minds off whatever ailed us. I was cooking dinner and to be honest imaging what it would be like to cook for the lightbulb man. Suddenly there was a burst of laughter from the girls followed by the doorbell.

I peepholed it and none other than Kevin aka the lightbulb man – was at my door. I opened the door, and he had flowers. He said, "I'm sorry if I came across as an asshole the other night. I'm really not one."

I laughed. "That was my impression, Kevin. But that's okay. You just are who you are!" I took the flowers, which were a mixture and beautiful.

" Are you busy?"

"My girls are here. We're just hanging out and having girls' night. I would invite you in, but they can be brutal."

"We won't be brutal—we promise!" Greta yelled out.

"Trust me," I said, "You don't want this right now! When are you back at the station?"

"Day after tomorrow. Call me tomorrow?" he asked.

"I will. And thanks." I closed the door while smelling my bouquet of flowers and smiling.

I turned around, and both girls were near nose to nose with me, clearly having peeped Kevin; now I had some explaining to do.

I gave them the whole story of how I first saw him at Lowe's, as the Lightbulb Man to finding out that he was a firefighter, Deputy Fire Chief, our dinner at the Bistro, as well as how he actually saw me first and was simply somewhat of an asshole with a bunch of flowers.

"Get to know him," Greta said, "It won't hurt to get to know him before you convince yourself that he's an asshole!"

We all returned and sat in our own comfy spots.

"He probably is an asshole!" Gabby blurted." You will probably be better off without him."

"I don't need any advice right now. I'm not trying to get to know him or not get to know him," I said. "I just want to live and not have a lot of drama in my life."

"Well, there's always going to be some sort of drama in every kind of relationship that exists with any man who breathes!" Gabby responded. "I am so over all men right now!"

"What are you bitter about right now?" I laughed. "Oliver at it again?"

"No. Oliver is not at it again. I'm just completely exhausted and I'm not trying to recover. I'm done with men. Travis was the one for me and he's gone. I just can't understand sometimes why he had to go," Gabby lamented. "My life was exactly where I wanted it to be. I just don't get it. I had my perfect man and now after eight years of no intimacy, I chose Calvin! Just stupid!"

"That's a decision you made, Gabby. Why are you being so down on yourself? And after eight years, EIGHT YEARS! You should have been with more than one Calvin!" Greta said.

"Yes, but sometimes you get more than you bargained for…" Gabby took a deep breath and a sip of wine.

"So, he's still calling; hasn't got the picture yet?" I asked.

Gabby tried to find the words to share where she was right now, being tested for herpes and full of uncertainty for the next three weeks. She was quiet and unsettled. "I need something stronger than wine! What do you have in this place?"

I looked at her. "Get up and see. There's something in there stronger than wine for sure! But I'm not getting it for you. You better get up!"

"That is not a problem!" Gabby went into the kitchen and checked the cabinets.

"It's not a bad thing to give love a chance," Greta said. She then paused and shared, "I'm staying with Cameron. I love him. I believe he loves me. I don't want to live without him in my life. I want us to raise our child and even more children. I love him, he made a mistake. Should we all have to pay for it, should our family cease to exist because of it? Right now, my answer is no."

Gabby snuggled up in her chair with a glass of something and something. "I heard that, Greta. And I think that's good. I really do," she said, taking a sip. "Does he know yet?"

Gabby wanted to share her pain, but she could not bring herself to tell her best girls because of the stigma that even she believed about herself.

"I haven't told him yet." Greta answered. "I will probably let him suffer a little more. He is really giving me the royal treatment, but I have eased up on him a bit."

"Is he out of the guest bedroom?" I asked.

"Not yet...but close!" Greta said.

Searching YouTube for a change, we found vintage comedians and started to listen again. (I want to interject here that I believe that comedians are the most incredibly important people on the planet. Just saying!) Pretty soon, even though we were all going through something, we were laughing to no end.

Oliver decided to behave as normal as possible to ease some of the stress of the wait for the Gabby's test results. He never brought it up after her initial tearful share and he ensured that she never had to see Calvin. He made one simple change. Every morning he made her a hot cup of tea and served it to her in the office. This morning, though, he was making two cups.

He lightly knocked on her ajar office door, inviting her to the dining area, "Hey, come, have a cup of tea with me."

She looked at him; her first thought was "No". But she closed her laptop, got up, and then went to the dining room and sat near the window. She was looking at the sidewalk, thinking of peeking through the windows the first night she and Travis found the building. Oliver returned with their tea.

"Your tea, my lady!" Oliver said, faking an English accent and sitting across from her. They both smiled, Gabby—reluctantly.

"You have a beautiful smile, you know," Oliver said. "Beautiful smile, beautiful soul."

Stirring her tea and with a fading smile, Gabby felt compelled to say, "Thanks, Oliver. For everything."

"I haven't done anything."

"Yes, you have," she assured him. "You make me not want to give up."

"There's no reason to give up. You mean too much to too many," he said.

"So, what's your story, Oliver? You know my deepest secret right now, and I know very little about you."

"I don't really have a story. I just want to feed people, good food. I love creating new dishes and experimenting with different flavours, mixing cultures."

"Mixing cultures, huh."

"Absolutely. I think nothing tells God how much we love Him than embracing each other and our differences. I like different."

"Have you ever been in love?"

"Yes."

"And?"

Oliver stared into his cup of tea and gave a short, audible laugh. "Don't know yet…"

'What does that mean?" Gabby laughed.

"My story isn't finished yet. Let me see your hand," he said.

Gabby held her open palm to him. She knew that she was falling for him, and their connection seemed to be the only thing holding her together. Her hand felt good in his. "The answer is not in the palm of my hand, you know," she said.

"It could be. I can read palms, you know." he gently ran his fingers in the lines of her hand.

"Oh really? So, what do you see?"

He looked into her eyes and said quietly and simply, "Happiness." His eyes left hers as he saw Lynne coming through the doors. He left the table and went to her.

Gabby turned to them as she felt a strange need to watch the interaction. She positioned her back to the wall, so she could take a good inconspicuous look. Oliver and Lynne had a brief conversation that Gabby could not hear, and Oliver reached into his wallet and gave her cash. Lynne tiptoed up and kissed him, then headed out of the door. Gabby felt something in her chest rip apart.

Oliver rushed to her as to explain, but Gabby was heading back to her office.

"Gabby, wait…"

She stopped, turned and looked at him, then said, "Happiness, huh?"

"This is really complicated right now."

"No, it's not, Oliver. It just got really simple." Gabby got her purse and left without allowing Oliver to tell her one more word.

Gabby always found solace on the waterfront. But it seemed that this was too much. She found herself having the fight of her life with herself to not drive into the river.

How could she even think Oliver could be interested in her? How could any person be interested in a person with herpes? And how could she ever tell another person if she had it? How will her life ever have a loving relationship again that she had with Travis? How does this life even matter anymore? Her tears seemed endless. Death seemed a strong and viable option. She looked at the gearshift and slowly placed her hand on it.

Suddenly, there were three light taps on her driver side window. When she looked up, it was Oliver. She let the window down and resumed looking down, her face covered in tears. She calmly let go of the gearshift and looked up at Oliver.

"I followed you," he said. He opened her car door and knelt at her side as she sat. He put his left hand just above her left knee and his fingers came to rest on the inside of her inner but lower thigh. He attempted to turn her face toward him with his right hand, but she resisted, so he slowly caressed the back of her neck.

"Listen, Lynne and I have this history. And I feel obligated to her. I don't want to get into all the specifics right now. But I will if you want me too."

"Oliver, why are you here, right now?"

"Because you matter to me. Because I care, and I want to be here for you. Let me do that," he said in full sincerity. He again reached to raise her lowered head and turn it toward him. This time being successful. "Let me do that."

As they looked at each other and he again found himself wiping her tears, he leant in to kiss her, Gabby shook her head in 'no' and turned away. He did not give up. "Please!" he whispered.

She could not help but look at him. In his eyes, she could see that everything was truly okay.

The kiss was inevitable.

It had been a week since Greta decided to stay with Cameron. While she felt he knew by default—she had not left, and she was less and less disconnected from him, she still had not completely let him off the hook.

And she had not told him she was pregnant. While she had fought tooth and nail for him not to find out, she had now decided it was time. But how to do it? It was going to be tricky. Any mention of a baby and pregnancy would likely lead him to think of Lisa. And might even create an uncomfortable situation for them both. They had not discussed the 'Lisa' situation since the first time. It had been too hard. But Greta knew this man; she loved him, and she was willing to work through this with him.

When they arrived home, while they still sat in the car, Greta looked at Cameron and said, "I want a spinach, onion, pepper jack cheese and smoked turkey omelette and cinnamon toast for dinner. I want you to cook for me."

Surprised, but definitely happy to do it, Cameron said, "Okay!"

Sitting at the kitchen bar while Cameron made breakfast for dinner, Greta said, "We need to talk about the baby."

"I know," Cameron said, "I've come to a conclusion."

"What?"

"I've done some investigation and we can get in utero paternity testing. I haven't talked to Lisa about it. I had planned to talk to you first. But I want to do it."

"It still bothers me, Cameron. I trusted you so much…" Greta said.

"I'm going to make it up to you. I promise," he said, continuing to cook. "If you let me."

"And what if Lisa's baby is yours?"

"You know that I'm going to take care of it. And I told her that when she told me it was mine. But I also told her I was not in love with her, I told her that I'm in love with you and only you. Greta, I did not initiate what happened. That does not make me less wrong, because I didn't fight it either," he said.

"Clearly! Every time I think about it, I want to slap you silly and call you a jackass! I can't believe you put us on the line like that, Cameron. I don't know, I just don't understand."

"I know," he said, "I don't understand either. But I need you. I cannot imagine my life without you." He passed her the omelette and completed the cinnamon toast. He made the same breakfast dinner for himself and sat on the same side of the bar with her to eat. "I need you to tell me that you still love me. I need you to tell me that you still want to be my wife. I know you may not be able to say it now—but I need you to tell me not to give up on us. I need you to say it."

Greta interrupted, "I still love you and still want to be your wife." She turned her swivel bar stool to face him; she put her hand on his and said, "When I said we need to talk about the baby, I was talking about our baby; Cameron, I'm pregnant."

Cameron was stunned for a moment. "You're pregnant?" He attempted to compose himself as he waited for confirmation.

"Yes, I am," Greta whispered.

Cameron began shaking his head, placed it over her shoulder and cried, saying "Thank you baby." And "I love you" over and over again.

Chapter 13

Today was one of the rare uneventful days at work. We had enough staff, a moderate amount of cases, no upset surgeons and no delays! We were even 100% for on-time first start cases! I really felt great. I headed home on time, and I was just going to relax out in the patio with ice-cold lemonade and rest my brain while listening to my favourite mixed playlist.

As I headed toward my building, I heard someone calling my name. I turned around, and yes sir! There he was, Kevin, heading home too. I didn't text him after the flowers, and we hadn't seen each other since.

"Hey," I said as I waited for him to catch up to me.

"So, how are you?" he asked.

"I'm good."

He leant in and kissed me on the cheek. Okay.

"I think I've missed you," he said with an awkward, surprised-at-the-fact smile.

We stood briefly. "Oh, really? You think?" I said. "You seem surprised!"

"I am," he said, "a little."

"Why? I am miss-able you know!" I laughed.

"Yes, you are, but you don't seem to want to be missed, not by me anyway!"

"And what are you basing that opinion on? What makes you think that?" I didn't get why he thought that. I might have been working too hard to keep from falling too hard.

A loud, obviously displeased voice, rapidly approaching us said, "So I guess this is your new thang, huh?" She looked at me up and down. "So, this is what you are leaving me for!"

"Wow!" I said, looking at Kevin.

"Wow, What, Bitch?" said this female—clearly old enough to know better than to make a public scene, dressed in leggings and a tank top, with very long blue braids, and most noticeably, a nose piercing with a chain on it (who does that at our age?); her body could take the outfit, but her attitude was super jacked up (just saying)—then looked at me as though she had an interest in fighting.

Kevin intervened, "Michele, why are you here, and how do you know where I live!"

"Michele," I said, "I don't know you. I don't know him, and I promise you, I don't want to know him!" I looked back at Kevin, "Enjoy your life."

As I walked away, I could hear a fairly heated discussion between the two of them. Something about her stalking him.

I went inside, made me a glass of ice-cold lemonade, still went out on my balcony and listened to my gospel playlist. Can't steal my joy!

I was not ten good minutes into relaxing, and the doorbell rang. I decided not to answer, but when it's followed by knocking, I got up.

The light bulb man… of course.

I opened the door.

"I have no idea why you are here!" I said, laughing.

"Are you going to invite me in?" he inquired.

"That depends."

"Upon what?"

"Whether or not the *lovely* Michele is somewhere lurking in the shadows!" I continued to laugh.

"She doesn't have access to this building," he said, walking past me.

"Lemonade?" I offered.

He nodded 'yes', and I poured and gave him the glass of ice-cold lemonade while motioning toward the balcony. We sat at the small two-seater table I had for times that I liked to eat outside. I started laughing again.

He looked at me square in the eyes, and as I struggled to remain in my seat and in my clothes, I heard him saying, "I like you." He paused and said again with fervour, "I really like you."

"You don't know me," I scoffed.

"I like what I know of you. And I want to know more," he confessed.

"You think you do," I said. "But what if I'm not the person you think you see?"

"I want to find out," he said.

He smelled so good. I didn't know what cologne he had on, but it made me want to bury my face somewhere along the side of his neck and kiss it slowly and methodically.

"I don't think I want to know you, Kevin. You have more than just baggage; you have mad, stalking, still in love with you and 'I will fight you *and* her' baggage! I don't need that in my life right now." I somehow managed to protest.

"Our divorce was finalised today. I really hate you saw that. And by the way, part of that was what I was trying to explain to you when you called me an asshole!" He quickly reminded me. "I don't want to spend time with you talking about my ex-wife. And I'm not. I came over because I wanted to tell you something."

Curious, I asked, "And what is that?"

"I like you."

"You've already told me that. Besides, this is crazy to me!"

"Why! Because I like you? Or because I'm telling you that I like you?" he asked.

"Both," I said.

"I'm not saying that I'm in love with you, Giselle! And I'm definitely not saying that I want to marry you," he assured me. "I'm saying…" he took a deep sigh, calmed himself and said in a quieter tone, "I'm saying, I like you. I see something when I see you. I knew it the first time I saw you. Not the first time I spoke to you, *the first time I saw you.* Even from a distance. And the more I see you, the more I want to see you. I feel something, something different. I don't know what it is exactly. But I want to know. I'm not saying date me if that's not something that you can do right now. I'm saying, maybe have dinner and go to a movie or the park a couple of times a week. And figure this out, at least, give it a chance."

I stood and looked over the 5th-floor balcony. I knew without any doubt whatsoever that I liked this man. I'd been inundated with thoughts of him since I saw him for the first time. And his green eyes and enticing aroma had me on the verge of yelling for him to take me!

Why am I so reluctant to move forward?

Oh yeah, the *lovely* Michele for one! And by lovely, I mean exceedingly not!

He rose and drew near to me. I turned to face him.

"It's okay, you know. It's safe," he said.

I couldn't continue to look into his eyes. Jesus! He smelled so good. I looked away.

"Giselle… Giselle," he said.

I looked at him, and he pulled me close to him. He looked at the strands of my hair that the wind had blown into my face and slowly moved them back while whispering to me, "Giselle, what are you thinking?"

"I don't know," I fabricated. 'I'm thinking I want you inside of me, moving, slowly, with great care, passion and emotions. I want you so bad!' I thought. My God, he smelled so good!

He kissed me, his mouth still fresh, cool and just a little sweet from the lemonade he had been drinking.

Damnit! That was good!

We kissed more, deeper, with greater passion. I could feel that he wanted me; I felt his growth against me.

"No!" I pushed him away. "You have to go."

He looked puzzled but stepped away.

I walked him to the door.

"Get your girl straight," I urged him and gave him a soft kiss on the lips.

I opened the door and as he slowly left; he looked down at his situation then back at me as if to say 'What are we going to do about this?'—but stayed silent.

I ushered him fully out of the door saying, "Good evening, Kevin."

Gabby had been working hard not to think of the results of the test. She and Oliver were connected on a different level—and to her, a horrific one. She kept asking herself why she shared this with him of all people. Not even her girls knew, but Oliver did. He was not using it in any harmful way, to be honest, he seemed more like a caring partner, supportive and loving, than someone who knew her deepest secret. It was as though they both were waiting for the results.

Oddly enough, she found herself wanting to spend more time with him. He's warm, funny and good to be around. And she also knew that she mattered to him. He told her that she did, he showed her that she did, and that mattered to her.

The day was coming to an end and Gabby was changing her shoes when Oliver came to the office saying, "I'm glad you're still here. I need to show you something."

"Oh no! What is it, Oliver?"

"I have to show you."

Oliver walked out, and Gabby followed closely behind.

As they approached the small room in the back where the staff and volunteers took their breaks, Gabby first saw the flicker of a candle, then noticed a fully set table, white tablecloth and all.

"You need a distraction, and I need to cook a nice meal." He pulled her seat out, and she sat without hesitation, without a word.

Oliver walked out, returned with two fresh pear and ginger cocktails with a touch of hazelnut syrup and bourbon, along with an oyster tray topped with crispy bacon and a very light pickled dill sauce. He sat, reached across the table, took her hands and said grace, "Thank You, Father God, for the food we are about to receive to help nourish our bodies as You nourish our spirit. Thank You, Father, for just being God and having power over all things that come, over all things that go and for the mercy and favour You have upon our lives. Amen."

Gabby looked up and said, "Who are you!" and laughed. "You say grace like my mother!"

Suddenly, remembering something, Oliver said, "Oh! I forgot!"

He jumped up, got his personal tablet and started a playlist. The first song, *You're All I Need to Get By*—by *Marvin Gaye* and *Tammi Terrell.* He sat with an 'I know this is a good choice' look on his face and smiled broadly.

"Ooooohhh! I see! You got tunes!" Gabby laughed.

Oliver gave a quick nod and smiled saying, "I do!"

"What do you know about Marvin Gaye—old school Marvin Gaye at that!" Gabby prodded.

"I love all types of music! But especially early Motown. Music will never again be made like that. It's not even possible. Do you like it?" he asked.

"I love it!"

They chatted superficially and joked through the hors d'oeuvres, and Oliver served his main course of roast beef tenderloin with cognac butter and some carrot mash with crispy asparagus.

The playlist was killing. Big time hits from all the greats: Aretha, Diana Ross, The Delfonics, Al Green, Fontella Bass, Spinners and the Four Tops *Reach Out I'll Be There* started playing, and Oliver stood, extending his hand and said, "Let's dance."

Gabby instantly hesitated and gave a thought to say no. Then took his hand and rose.

They danced. They danced slower than the beat of the song. They embraced, so close. Oliver leant back to look into her eyes. Their eyes met in truth, deep truth and undeniable real love. Their foreheads touched and noses met as they slowly swayed to the music. They each moved their cheeks across the others' and Oliver kissed her on the neck. He moved again as to kiss her but again placed his forehead on hers.

"I love you," he whispersed, "I've loved you from day one when we interviewed. I knew it was you." He continued to whisper, "I love you, Gabby."

"I love you, Oliver," Gabby confessed. "I don't know when I knew. But I've known before right now, before today, this week even. I do love you."

"I've hoped for a very long time that this moment would happen!" he said, exhaling in relief. He attempted to kiss her, but she did not allow it.

"I do love you, Oliver, and I've been thinking about that a lot lately," she said, pulling away and seating herself back at the dinner table. Tears started to fall with a steady flow down her cheeks. "The test results should be back any minute now, I checked already. They are late. What if I'm positive; what if I have it?"

"Then we will deal with it *together*."

She shook her head, "No." Continuously shaking her head, she said, "I won't do that to you. I won't."

Oliver knelt before her, placing his hands on her outer thighs and said, "You can't get rid of me that easily!"

Gabby took her napkin and wiped her eyes and her face. "I mean it, Oliver. I see you, in a weird Avatar type of way. You are a hugely beautiful, caring and loving man. You deserve so much, so much that is beautiful like you…and clean," she pulled away from him saying, "Not tainted like me." The tears rolled…

"Listen," Oliver said, "I've had almost as much time to think about this as you have. And I have thought about it. Over and over again. And you know what? A positive test is not enough for me to give you up! I've done research too. Do you know how many millions of people are living with herpes? And most of them have no symptoms at all. Many of them don't even know it! There is medication, this is not a death sentence or a sentence that says you have to be alone the rest of your life!"

She was still shaking her head. "I'm not going to do that to you." She continued tearful, "you deserve better than me. I'm not a good choice." She dropped her head in shame.

Oliver immediately raised her head back up and looked into her eyes saying, "There is *NO* better than you. None whatsoever! And I'm telling you right now, don't even try it!

I'm not going anywhere. I'm in for the long haul, regardless of what it is." He kissed her, and she kissed him back.

Cameron had done research on in utero paternity testing. He had yet to get Lisa to agree and was concerned that she would not. Greta had decided not to interfere, interact or in any way be a part of whatever happened between Cameron and Lisa before the baby was born.

She was more concerned about the safety and health of her own baby, and to be honest, she was not sure that under the same circumstances as Lisa, she would do in utero paternity testing. She knew Cameron had some concerns, but they were his to deal with.

Lisa decided to have a conversation with Greta about the entire situation. Though Greta had been determined not to have that discussion, she changed her mind, even against her better judgement and agreed to talk with her in the park across from Calibri's.

It was a beautiful day in the park. The sun was shining, the sky was blue, and there were just enough fluffy white clouds to cast momentary shadows while passing over. Being outside was one of Greta's favourite things, and while she wasn't sure why Lisa wanted this mysterious meeting, she felt some weird obligation to go. Lisa was off, and they were meeting at noon.

(This meeting Greta was on time for!)

Lisa walked up, smoking a cigarette.

"Smoking while you're pregnant is an interesting choice," Greta said without even considering if it was the right thing to say.

"Don't judge me!" Lisa shot back, "I'm trying to do something for you!"

"Okay. I'm sorry. Maybe I should not have said that. I apologise," Greta said. "But I have a problem with smoke…"

"We're outside! Where do you want me to go? Forget it!" She dropped the cigarette on the ground and extinguished it with her foot. "Okay. Can we talk?" Lisa was a little rough around the edges, to say the least. She never had a problem speaking up or going for what she wanted. Truth is, she had been working on Cameron's attention for weeks before he broke. She was attractive and in her mid-twenties but unsettled. She wanted something; she was not sure how to get. She waited for Greta's answer before sitting.

"Sure," Greta said.

Lisa joined Greta on the park bench and looked around as though she was securing the area.

"I've been thinking," Lisa started, "I really don't want a baby right now. But I can't afford to get an abortion. I was thinking that maybe you could help me. I know you don't want to start your marriage with a husband and a new-born stepchild."

"How do you know that?" Greta asked.

"I wouldn't," she said. "I can really tell that Cameron is a good man. I know he will make a good husband. He has already told me that whatever I and the baby need, he will do. But I feel a little bad for you."

"That's an interesting position to take," Greta said, doubtful of Lisa's sincerity.

"You're welcome," Lisa popped a piece of gum in her mouth and chewed as though the antidote to all her problems were hidden somewhere deep within and she had to chew it out. "I just don't need a baby right now."

"Did you talk to Cameron about this?"

"Not yet," she said. "You know he really wants this baby."

"You should talk to Cameron." Greta was done with the conversation. "I'm going to go."

"No, wait!" Lisa exclaimed. "Just think about it a couple of days. But don't tell Cameron. Not yet, okay?"

Greta stood and looked at her, shaking her head and walking away. "Think about not smoking as long as you are pregnant! Okay?"

Greta went back and finished her shift. She did not tell Cameron what Lisa wanted, and he was smart enough not to ask. The night went by fast, and Greta found herself awake very early the next morning, wondering what manner of predicament Lisa had put her in and how to handle it.

Chapter 14

Gabby and Oliver left The Kitchen and went to her place after dinner the night before. They decided to stay the night together, and while they did not have sex, it was perhaps the single best night of Gabby's life since Travis died. She slept in his arms all night, and he just held her. She woke up and moved from time to time, and he would just hold her closer. The love between the two of them was amazing. She needed this so much.

She woke up before he did and just watched him asleep, felt him breathe for a few minutes. She then eased her way out of the bed, careful not to wake him. She went downstairs and made breakfast. She grabbed her phone, downloaded Marvin Gave and Tammie Terrell and woke him to, *You're All I Need to Get By.* He opened his eyes and sat up. Gabby set the bed tray across him complete with orange juice, a large glass of milk, a small sugar bowl, and honey nut cheerios, for two.

"Cheerios!" He laughed. "The first meal you cook for me is cheerios!" He pulled her toward him.

"*Honey nut* Cheerios! Don't get it twisted now. Give me my props!"

They kissed.

No fear.

No worries.

Their song was on repeat…

Still a workday, Gabby jumped in the shower first.

"Knock, knock…"

"Oliver?" Gabby, somewhat surprised, asked.

"Can I come in?"

"NO!" she laughingly screamed.

"Are you sure?"

"NO! I mean YES! Get away!" She continued to laugh.
"You're going to regret this later today!" he teased.
"I regret it already!"
"Me too!" he said, walking away from the door.
And the song played on…

The girls were meeting for lunch today. There's so much going on in everyone's life. It might take lunch and dinner. But I refused to be the first one today. We were supposed to meet at noon; I decided to be there at 12:30!

Okay, how on earth was that possible that I was 30 minutes late and neither of them had arrived? We couldn't even meet at Chick-Fil-A and be on time! If I didn't want to talk about the *lovely Michele*, I would leave! For goodness sake!

I saw Gabby driving up, and before she could get in, Greta came. I was fortunate walking in as a table got emptied near the door, and I grabbed it instantly. Once we all had our food, we settled down to talk.

I started, "I am so baffled right now. I don't know what to do about Kevin."

"Date him! Get some sex!" Greta quickly advised.

"Greta! Having sex is not always the answer to every question!" Gabby jumped in.

"I know that. But I will bet it's the answer to this one! This girl hasn't had sex this decade! Maybe even the last two decades!" Greta added, defending her position.

"I'm sitting here, you know!" I reminded them. "And just so you know, I met the former *Mrs* Kevin Harper."

"How?" they both asked in stereo surround sound.

"Well, apparently their divorce was finalised, and she saw him somewhere and followed him home. He was talking to me in the parking lot, and she confronted not only him but me as well!"

"Whoa!" Gabby said. "Definitely don't sleep with him. Whoever you sleep with for the first time is going to own you! He is going to have you, so mind-blown. You are not going to be able to contend with a crazy ex-wife. You will be as crazy as she is!"

They decided to take turns roasting me—

"Yeah, you might be out there, cat-fighting!"

"And on YouTube!"

"And on the news, 'Nurse manager in street fights with boyfriend's ex-wife!'"

"Are you two done yet?" I asked, not particularly seeing the humour in all of that.

They stopped laughing and looked at me.

"I really don't know what to do," I said.

Greta asked me very simply, "What do you want to do?"

I thought for a second or two. "I want to go back to who I was before I ever saw the light bulb man!"

"Well," Gabby said, "that's not an option."

"He said he liked me and wanted to get to know me," I added. "But you are right; I haven't been in a relationship for so long; I really don't know how to be in a relationship anymore! But mostly, I don't want any drama! I am responsible for too much; I can't be distracted with drama, : of any kind!"

"But you have to live too," Greta said earnestly.

"Proper work/life balance, right!" I added quietly. "I want to see that happen!"

"We're not going to solve your problem today!" Greta said, dismissing my issue as a non-issue. "My fiancé's baby's mama-to-be asked me to help her get an abortion! And asked me not to tell my fiancé!"

"Oh, she's special, huh? She must be kin to my *lovely* Michele!" I joked.

"Did you tell Cam?" Gabby asked.

"Not yet," she said, "but I am going to."

"Oh!" I remembered, "Did you tell him that you're pregnant?"

Greta smiled broadly, "I did. He was so overcome with happiness! He just cried like a baby himself! And he has been so amazing, I can't tell you."

"That means they will definitely be getting married!" Gabby looked at me and said laughing.

"We all knew that when she didn't kick him to the curb from the beginning!"

"You remember when Boss Man cheated on Bridget? She said she was not going to let some random no count break up her family, and she didn't!" Greta tossed in for good measure. "And you know Bridget was tough on some things. But she said infidelity is not good enough reason to let a good man go, and I agree."

"I always disagreed with that!" I interjected. "I honestly believe, and this is only for me, my man—if I ever get to that point—he will not be unfaithful. I know people can be faithful if they really want to be. I believe sometimes people just use bad judgement, make bad decisions. But if they really do not want to be unfaithful, then they won't. If they do, it's for a reason, that they have calculated will make them feel better."

Greta asked, "And you would let one mistake ruin your life, his life and make you all miserable?"

"It would not be me doing it. It would be him," I said, "that's what I think right now anyway. Maybe. I don't know!"

We all paused, taking sips of our drinks and bites of lunch.

"Okay, Gabby, Your turn!" I said.

"I may not want to share what's going on with me just yet," Gabby said pensively.

"That means it's juicy!" Greta declared, "Anytime you have to decide whether to talk about it or not, yeah…pretty juicy!"

Shaking her head, Gabby explained, "It's not that it's all that I mean." She shrugged and gave a slight facial grimace. "I may be living the worst-case scenario for my life moving forward *and* the best-case scenario for my life moving forward, all at the same time!" She shrugged and grimaced with 'and I really don't know' glance.

I suddenly thought I've got it. "You're in love with Calvin and you don't know how to tell your in-laws!"

"HELL NO!" she strongly emphasised.

"Okay!" I said, feeling like saying 'Yikes! That's not it.'

"Giselle, I don't know. I need to figure some things out and get more information," Gabby added.

"And you don't want to bounce it off your girls?" Greta asked, "That's what we do!"

Gabby looked at both of us and said quietly but matter-of-factly, "Not this," and shook her head while taking a sip of her drink.

Gabby felt tears welling up in her eyes and wiped them; she laughed because she thought about Oliver at the same time as she did her pending test results.

"It's crazy right now!" she said and laughed again through the tears.

Both Greta and I could see her distress. But we also understood her to need to get understanding herself before sharing. We reached to her from both sides and did a three-way hug. We didn't need full details to be supportive.

If Bridget were here, she would probably remind us how all pain is an opportunity for growth and that without it, we would become stagnant. She would say, "Even though you may not believe it, you are stronger than anything that comes upon you. Something will always come to knock you down and sometimes, guess what? You're going to fall. That's life. The winning is simply in getting back up and moving on. Sooner or later, the pain will either go away or become bearable. And sometimes, the thing that has you so messed up today is not even a memory a year from now. You just have to hold on." That was Bridget.

We weren't as good as Bridget, and I tried to think of something in the moment to say that was great like she used to say. Didn't happen.

"We are here for you whenever you are ready," I said.

"We love you, Gabby," Greta added.

She cried and laughed a little bit more and did our three-way hug a little bit longer.

Chapter 15

I was hanging out with Kevin tonight in his apartment. Truth was, being with him relaxed me. When I was around him, I didn't have to be strong, I didn't have to be in charge. I just had to be me.

Tonight, we planned to do two movies—one of my favourites and one of his. We won't tell each other until time to watch and we promised to watch and pay attention to the other's choice. We had pizza delivery planned for dinner and because neither of us cared much for alcohol, we stuck with water, tea or lemonade.

Again, I chose to dress down. I wore one of my black Adidas track pants, a tank top and flip flops. When I knocked on the door, I smelled something great, but both sweet and savoury. He opened the door but had on oven mitts and didn't wait for me to get in and close the door. Instead, he quickly headed back to the kitchen.

"Make sure you lock the door," he yelled back.

I locked the door and slowly made my way in. I was so shocked and tickled!

"Cookies!" I exclaimed, cracking up, "Really, dude? You're making cookies!" As he pulled the perfect snickerdoodles out of the oven and placed them on a cooling rack.

"Okay, because obviously, you are impressed! They are from store-bought sugar cookie dough. I rolled them in cinnamon sugar and baked them!" He said with a slight bit of pride though.

I looked about, and yes, I was impressed. This man had a spread that looked like a minor tailgating party!

"Tell me you did not prepare all of this!" I said in somewhat an awe.

"I did."

"But we were going to get pizza!" I said, slightly disappointed. I do not eat pizza very often; it is not my friend! But I love it anyway.

"Changed my mind. Didn't want pizza!" he said plainly. "I wanted wings, hot, garlic parmesean *and* lemon pepper—and yes, I made them all myself! I wanted fresh guacamole, so yes, I made fresh guacamole! I wanted to make both coleslaw and potato salad because I didn't know which one you liked." He stopped to explain, then continued, "I had to make a small garden salad at least—so there! Shoot me!"

I got tickled. I was so tickled I could barely breathe. "Wings, Kevin?" I laughed the words—"You probably don't even like hot wings!" I continued laughing.

"What?" He laughed too. "Why can't I like wings?"

"The true test is how does it taste?" I asked.

"Baby, I've got mad kitchen skills!" he bragged. "Just relax and let me run this!"

"Are we still watching movies?" I ask sarcastically.

"We are." He laughed. "Wine?"

"You just changed everything, huh?"

"Why not?" He laughed.

I sat at his bar while he plated the cookies, sipping the wine, looking at him and liking what I was seeing and feeling.

"I could see your mind working overtime!" he said, "What were you thinking?"

"Honestly?" I asked because he might not really want to know.

"Honestly," he answered, finishing the cookies and looking directly at me.

"I'm thinking…I like that you like me; I like the way you said that you like me," I said. I rolled my eyes a bit because I was a little disappointed in myself to admit it. "I like that you are a firefighter and I love the way you smell."

"That's good, right?" he inquired.

"Yes, well, maybe it's a bit too good," I added. "And you know what they say, 'if it seems too good to be true, it's probably not true'!"

"First of all," he said, pouring himself a glass of wine, "I'm not all that good! You said it yourself; I'm an asshole!"

"Tell me something about yourself that's not great, something really crappy or that maybe other people say is crappy."

"That's easy!" he said and took a sip of his wine and leant back on the counter. "I literally *hate* clingy, jealous women with no confidence in anything that they do! I can't stand a woman begging me for money or things while she lays around and does nothing. I think everybody should work; everybody should have a purpose, I hate *lazy*—or what I feel is lazy. Some people, mostly people who are like that, don't like me for feeling that way about it!"

"Boy, you might be an asshole for real!" I said after he laid *that* out on the line!

"Why? Don't get me wrong!" he explained. "I really know how to support and treat my woman. *And...*" he changed his tone a bit to let me know he was talking directly to me, "*I love taking care of my woman.*" He took another sip of wine while continuously looking at me for a response.

I didn't really react.

"What movie did you choose?" I asked, changing the subject. I know it's probably something to separate me from my underpants! Not going to happen, buster!

"Tombstone," he said.

"Tombstone?" I almost gasped. That's not going to get me out of my underwear! What does he mean by Tombstone? I asked myself.

"You like Westerns, I hope," he said, semi-asking.

"Actually, Kevin, I do," I said, and I really do.

But in my mind, I was thinking but not for tonight! Now I had to change my movie! No more *Love and Basketball*! Which was my all-time favourite movie, ever! Man! I was going to pick something so random now!

"I'm thinking about *American Hustle*. Have you seen it?" I asked. Gotcha!

"Hmmm, not yet. It's old, right?" he asked. He was expecting *Love and Basketball!*

"Well, 2013," I said.

"Okay, let's start with that. Or do you want to start with Tombstone?"

"I've seen them both," I said. "So, let's do the one you haven't seen yet," I said. All the time, I was thinking, I know I got you!

American Hustle was great! I knew that! He loved it! The food was fantastic. Now we were watching *Tombstone*, and Kurt Russell just slapped the blood out of Billy Bob Thornton and asked him if he was just going to stand there and bleed! We both loved that! Watching this movie, right now with the Light Bulb Man AKA Kevin Harper, Deputy Fire Chief...I was *happy*.

At home, that night, Greta decided to talk to Cameron about Lisa and their conversation in the park. They'd had dinner and were washing dishes together in the old-fashioned way. They had a dishwasher, but this was one of the things they liked doing together. As Cameron washed, she stood next to him with her back to the sink.

"I want to tell you something I was asked not to tell you," she said.

"Okay," he said, continuing to wash the dishes.

"Lisa asked me to help her get an abortion. She also asked me not to tell you."

He stopped washing the dishes, dried his hands and continued to hold the towel.

"Really?" he asked, surprisingly, not surprised.

"You don't seem surprised," she said.

"I've made it clear to her that I will do everything for *my* child. But I must have a paternity test. I asked for the in utero test. We can have the results in three to five days. Which means we can know before you and I are married. She gets it," he said.

"You don't believe it's yours, do you?" she probbed.

"No, that's not it," he said. "Not really it at all. But it runs the risk of coming between us or affecting us, you and me. I need to know with certainty that it's my child."

Somewhat taken aback, Greta said, "Cam, I would never try to come between you and your child! How could you think that?"

"I don't believe that you would ever do that, certainly not intentionally. But I do believe that the stress of raising a child, especially under, well, unusual circumstances can be taxing. If that can happen, I don't need to find out that it's not my child. I need to *know* that it is," he said.

"Wow!" Greta responded, "I don't know what to say. But I know you're doing what you think is the right thing."

Bright and early Monday morning, and it was time for the delivery from the farm. Oliver had already told Gabby he would take care of it, and she remained in the office.

Calvin and his team made the delivery and Oliver signed off. No words at all had been exchanged. Calvin initially headed out, then stopped and walked toward Oliver.

"Man," Calvin said, "I think we somehow got off on the wrong foot. I don't want to do that." He extended his hand.

Oliver hesitated, then accepted Calvin's handshake. "No problem, man."

"I don't really know what happened between us, man." Calvin began to explain.

Oliver interrupted, "Hey, don't worry about it, but I really have a lot to do. See you next delivery."

"What is your problem, man!" Calvin quickly asserted.

Refusing to engage him, Oliver said, "There's no problem. I just have work to do."

"Well, can you get Gabby for me?"

"She's not available."

Calvin took a big sigh as he watched Oliver walking away and said, "Son of a …", then left in a huff.

Chapter 16

Calibri's was hoping for the lunch hour, and Lisa was being overly sweet and kind to Cameron and the exact opposite to Greta. Greta wasn't so sure why, but she had not trusted Lisa from the moment she found out about the pregnancy.

Greta also was not feeling well, still, she worked hard to assist the team through the noon rush. But she became extremely nauseated, then light-headed and nearly passed out, being caught by a male waiter just before she hit the floor. He lifted her and took her into Cameron's office and laid her on the office sofa.

Cameron ran to her side. "Are you okay?"

Tommy came with a cold cloth and placed it on her forehead. "Do we need to call an ambulance?"

Random staff members started to stick their heads in the office to see how Greta was doing, including Lisa.

Cameron asked again, "Are you okay, baby?"

Holding the cold cloth on her forehead and keeping her eyes closed, she said, "Yes. I'm okay."

"Do you need me to call the doctor? Do we need to check the baby?" Cameron asked.

"I'm okay, baby," she said, "and the baby is okay too. I just got dizzy and nauseated. That's normal."

"Of course, she's pregnant!" Lisa shouted! "Of f...ing course!" Lisa laughed. "Well isn't that just precious?"

Cameron turned to Lisa and said, "Please leave this office and return to work, Lisa!"

"Why didn't you tell me she was pregnant, Cameron?" she shot back!

"Because you are not a factor in our lives! It's none of your business!" He was angry, then he calmed himself. "Please go back to work, Lisa."

"You said that you love our child and that you were going to take care of us!"

"Tommy," Cameron said, "take the staff back to the floor. Lisa, come in. Close the door."

Tommy and the others left the office; Lisa sat in a random chair farthest away from Greta, who by this time had sat up from a vulnerable position to see what was really going on but kept the cold cloth against her forehead.

Cameron looked at Lisa. "What are you trying to do? Yes, if that is my child, I will love it, protect and care for it to the ends of the earth. But I have told you I want an in utero paternity test, we can get results in five days or less. And even if we don't get it now, before I do anything paternal—I want a blood test."

"Why because now that she's pregnant, you don't need my baby?" Lisa asked with indignation. "Your precious Greta! Do you know she tried to get me to get an abortion? She said she would pay for it! She wanted to kill your child! You need to know that!"

Greta had heard enough. She dropped the cool cloth. Slowly got up from the sofa, checked her balance and headed for the door.

"Greta, wait!" Cameron said.

She looked at him. "It's okay. I need a minute." She walked out and closed the door behind herself.

"I love you, Cameron." Lisa said, "We can be a strong family."

"No, we cannot. I was wrong, I was weak, I made a mistake. I've told you that repeatedly. I love Greta. But I promise you, I will take care of our child and help you raise it. But I need you to stop this. Greta is going to be my wife."

"But she wants to kill our baby. She tried to pay for an abortion!"

Greta returned with her cell phone in her hand.

"Why, Lisa, would I ever want you to have an abortion, why?" Greta asked.

"Because you want Cameron all to yourself. You want us completely out of the picture! You are nothing nice, not like he thinks!"

Greta just looked at her for a moment, then looked at her phone and scrolled a bit, then hit 'play'.

On came full audio of their conversation in the park.

"I recorded you, bitch! I never trusted you!" Greta said, eyebrows raised and informing, yet calm and collective.

Lisa listened to ensure that she was fully exposed. Once she heard herself in full light, caught lying to discredit Greta, she stood and stormed out of the office.

Lisa went to the female employee locker room and was gathering her things when her best friend co-worker, Jewel, walked in.

"You told me a long time ago whose baby this is, and it wasn't Cameron's. I know, and you know. Then suddenly, you tell me you have a plan to get someone to take care of you and your 'no good ex's baby' for the rest of your lives. This is not right, Lisa. They are both good people. If you don't set it straight, I will."

"Fine, Jewel!" Lisa yelled. "Do it!"

"If you don't," Jewel said, "I will. You've got three days. Friday morning, I'm telling them both." She returned to service.

Today was another banner day in the OR. I think part of being a nurse is that we sacrifice ourselves for others. A major case in point—I do not know a single nurse, including myself, who goes to the bathroom as soon they realise that the need exists. We always wait until that moment either just before our bladders rupture or they involuntarily relieve themselves. I've seen more nurses running to the bathroom than running for their pay cheques!

Speaking of bathrooms, the worst is when you really need to go, run in, and someone has just dropped a number two! But you have to go, so you try to live through it. You get out as quickly as you possibly can because the stench is killing you. Opening the door, there is someone waiting who is going to think it was you! I always hate that, but I digress.

I was asked today, when I consider the high degree of difficulty associated with my job, do I sometimes think it's not worth the payoff of taking care of other people. I said that is what keeps me going. Knowing that every single day my team and I are going to make a difference in the lives of others. Not many people wake up in the morning, knowing that their day will consist of making someone's life better. I often say to the team, "Right now, as we speak, someone is in pain, someone is scared, someone is praying, and their family and friends are praying. And most importantly, they are going to be placed in our hands. We are God's hands. How do we answer those prayers?"

We were crazy busy today. And I had the pleasure of dealing with a specific surgeon throwing tantrums like a little kid. That's not unusual. A tiny few have watched too much television and think they are surgeons in a TV series. They are the stars of their show and they must have their on-screen time. Anything that throws them off script can be catastrophic to their fragile egos and everybody around them.

But we made it through today—with mandatory overtime, but we made it.

Interestingly enough, I didn't want to go home and crash. I wanted to surprise Kevin and pop by the fire station. That was never a good idea, surprising a man. Especially when you don't know where you stand with him *and you know he has a crazy ex!* But I did that anyway.

The fire truck was outside; some guys were washing it. I saw him standing there, talking with the guys and eased in slowly. I was going to back out and turn around if it felt weird. But he looked toward me and walked over to the car.

"I thought that was you!" I said, all bold like this just happened to happen. Fake as I can be. I knew I was looking for him! And I knew where he would be. I didn't want to tell him I was feeling a strong need to see him, so I came looking!

"Hey!" He had a big smile on his face. "I was just thinking about you."

He leant in the car window and kissed me. "I will see you tonight." He stepped away. My need was fulfilled. I backed out and a car horn blew really loudly! Nearly scared the crap out of me!

Just as I got square in the car heading away, the phone rang. It was Kevin.

"Hey, baby," he said, "the car that just blew, it was Michele."

"I know you're kidding me!" I said in disbelief.

"No. It was her. Look, I'll see you tonight," he said.

"Don't bother!" I said quite pissed and hung up the phone. He did not call me back.

But, as I was driving, it looked like I was being followed. Okay, I figured I was just tripping because of what just happened. I didn't remember the car, but I kept thinking it's her. Then the sensible me took over and I said I knew this woman was not following me! I was really being silly! I headed home—still pissed.

And you know what? I was done with him! He was, without a doubt, more trouble than he's worth! And I didn't even care. It was against my better judgement to go by there anyway. I just wanted to go home, binge-watch *The Office* and indulge in some black raspberry ice cream.

I was out of my car heading in when a car pulled up in front of me and cut me off. Yes. The same one that was following me. Yes. Michele.

"So, it is you!" she snorted.

"You know," I said, "if you would give him a chance to miss you, maybe you could get him back! You keep following him and making him angry. That's not going to make him want you. That's going to make him want to get away from you!" I was very honest and not threatened or threatening; I just told her the truth. "If you want him, if you want a chance, you've got to not make him hate you and your behaviour. Nobody wants to be around *crazy!* And right now, you are acting crazy. Just so you know."

She looked at me as though she got it. She didn't say another word. She let her window up and left.

I was more pissed than I was at first. I thought I will never see or talk to him again. This was too much. I knew this would be nothing but trouble! And I really liked him a lot.

Damn it!

Actually, I was going to speak to him one more time! I called him.

"Your girl just followed me home and confronted me!" I informed him.

"What?" he was surprised. "Are you okay?"

"I'm okay," I said, reflecting. "Listen, Kevin. You've got unfinished business. I don't know—it may be even dangerous. So, here's the thing. I'm going to need you to leave me alone. Take care of your business. Please don't call me anymore. Please don't call me, come by, pass notes under my door or in any way contact me again. Goodbye."

I hung up the phone, and just like that, it's all over.

Chapter 17

Today was Friday. It'd been well over the three weeks and the initial results of the herpes test were still not in, and somehow it had slipped Gabby's mind. She and Oliver were at a very beautiful place in their relationship and were prepping together when the phone rang. Gabby didn't assume or even consider that the call could be regarding the test.

"Hello," she answered.

"This is she," pausing and listening.

She pulled a rolling stool that was just near her and sat, continuing to listen. "Are you sure?"

She paused briefly. "What should I do, when should I come back in?" she asked.

"Okay. Thank you. I will see you then," Gabby hung up the phone and dropped her face into her hands.

Oliver ran to her. "It's okay, baby. We will handle it together! It's okay!"

She looked up to his strongly concerned and supportive eyes looking at her as though he loved her more than ever. "I'm negative," she said. "I don't have it!"

Oliver instinctively grabbed her up off the stool and swept her off her feet in a twirling embrace sealed with a joyous kiss!

They heard a voice, "Now it makes sense, white boy! Now I know what your problem was!" Calvin had come in from the front. The kitchen was still open for late-comers, and he walked in and went looking for Gabby.

"Leave, Calvin," Gabby said.

Oliver shook his head to Gabby. "Let me handle this," he said. Oliver pushed Gabby behind him and said to Calvin.

"Look, man, why don't you just leave? You're trespassing. You need to go."

"Or what?" Calvin huffed. "Oh. You're going to call the police! Hoping they will come to kill me! That's what white people do now. Murder by the police! That's so like white people!"

"I'm asking you to leave; none of us wants any trouble," Gabby said.

"No. You don't want trouble; all you want is this trash!" Calvin blurted, "Tell me, did you go to the doctor? Did you get your test? Do you have herpes?" attempting to embarrass her.

"Now you're out of line!" Oliver angrily interjected.

"NO!" I DO NOT HAVE HERPES!" Gabby full-on shouted.

"I know you don't, bitch! I lied! You think you are so much better than me, all the time letting me screw your brains out without a rubber, on the first night! You tramp!"

Hearing the ruckus coming from the prep area, random men from the dining room came to investigate.

Oliver walked up to Calvin.

Calvin quickly shoved Oliver in the chest.

Oliver instinctively swang a very hard right that landed on Calvin's chin, and with that, one punch knocked Calvin out cold.

Four of the men picked Calvin up and headed out of the front door with him. He awakened, attempting to fight. They put him down and two of the men pinned him against the wall outside of the building.

One other came face to face with him and said, "You're in the wrong place, my man. You're not going to disrespect Miss Gabby, and you're not going to fight our cook. I don't think you know what you're doing, but I've got nothing else to lose." He looked firmly into Calvin's eyes. "Never come here again. Never."

They let Calvin go, and he quickly left. He later quit his job at the farm. Not sure where he ended up.

Lisa had not returned to Calibri's since the outburst earlier in the week. Jewel, her best friend had given her until today, to tell the truth about the baby, or Jewel would tell Cameron and Greta the truth.

Cameron and Greta assumed she had quit, but were waiting for her return, knowing that she was pregnant and would need assistance.

Greta was acting Hostess when Lisa arrived and automatically became defensive. But attempted not to show it.

"Hi, Greta," Lisa said, "do you think I could talk with you and Cameron?"

"Okay. Give me a minute," Greta said and picked up the phone to call Cameron.

Lisa sat momentarily and noticed another staffer coming to relieve Greta.

Both Lisa and Greta headed to the office where Cameron was waiting.

Cameron stayed seated at the desk, and Greta leant against the wall behind him. Lisa took a seat in front of the desk and there was an awkward silence.

Lisa started, "When I first found out I was pregnant, it made me sick. I remember thinking that it's hard enough to take care of myself, how could I take care of a baby?" She laughed. "And the baby's daddy! I knew I could never depend on his sorry ass. When you came in that Saturday, I was just looking for a way out. I kept thinking about how great it would be if you were my baby's daddy. I knew you were a really nice and caring guy. I could tell you were really messed up about something. My first thoughts were just to help you. Then I thought if I could just get you to do it, I would be set up. It was hard to seduce you, but when you finally gave in, I knew I was set for life. But I didn't know how close you two were." She squirmed a bit in the chair. "I'm sorry. It's not your baby, Cameron, it never was. I needed help."

A few moments of awkward silence and relief.

"Why didn't you just ask for help?" Cameron asked.

"I couldn't. I haven't been here long. You guys don't know me. Why would you help me for no reason? I felt like if you thought it was your baby you would have to help me. And wow! You went way beyond what I thought. You were so supportive of me and the baby. And all you wanted was the one thing I could never do—a paternity test. I didn't know you were pregnant, Greta, but I thought Cameron, if I could make you break up with her about my baby, you would forget the pregnancy test. But," she continued looking at Greta, "you outsmarted me and recorded our conversation. So, I'm sorry."

Silence in the room.

Greta asked, "What are you going to do now?"

"I don't know," said Lisa, shaking her head and looking down.

"Well," Greta said, "I don't think you should quit your job until you figure things out a bit better. Right, Cam?"

Hesitantly, Cameron responded, "Right."

"I still have a job here?"

"You do," They both said together and then looked at each other.

"Thanks," Lisa said. She stood and headed to the door. She turned back and looked at Greta and Cameron and said, "I'm sorry."

"Lisa, wait," Greta walked over to her. "Don't keep saying you're sorry. This was not your fault alone. That's what's true. There's a lot that I don't like about all of this, but I want you and your baby to be okay. And I want you to know that you are not wholly responsible."

"Thanks for that," Lisa said and left.

Lisa worked at Calibri's six more weeks.

Greta and Cameron's wedding was absolutely beautiful and the weather was perfect at the Botanical Gardens. But this strapless, tea length, Cinderella at the ball, coral bridesmaid dress was not making me happy. I couldn't wait to get out of it! I told Greta I did not want a strapless dress! But nooooo! And now I was mentally exhausted because I spent most of the evening afraid my boobs were going to pop out!

Well, at least, now I could go inside and get comfortable—you would think!

Just as I stepped my foot out of the car, I had a visitor. I completed my move out of the car and stood near the hood.

"I've been waiting for you." Standing there in living colour with bright orange hair, torn army green booty shorts and a too-small green camouflage tank top showing her navel was the *not lovely but crazy, Michelle.* She was apparently ready for battle.

I was already pissed because of the dress I was wearing, and if I didn't mention it earlier, my feet hurt in those heels! I leant against the hood, took my heels off and crossed my arms holding them. "Okay…" I didn't crack a smile and looked directly at her.

Michelle put her hands on her hips and she was breathing hard. "I want you to know you can't have my husband. I want you to know that you need to back up! I'm not playing with you; if you don't want some real trouble, you better forget everything you know about my husband!"

Is this chick ready to fight me over some man I am not even seeing? Okay, I'll bite! I thought.

"And your husband is who?"

"You know who my husband is, bitch! Don't play that dumb shit with me!" She angrily blew back.

I placed my shoes on the hood of my car and eased my hand into my purse and easily located my pepper spray. I was concerned about flying boobs, but my plan was she won't see for a week because I was going to empty this can in her eyes!

"Okay, three things. One, I am not a bitch; and two, I am not seeing your husband or to be more exact, your ex-husband, and last but certainly not least, I am not the one—so go play crazy with somebody else!" I could feel my breathing increasing, and I was getting angrier by the second. But I spoke very matter-of-factly. I didn't raise my voice and I maintained my position leaning against the hood of my car.

"I'm not crazy!" she screamed (which is always a clear indication that the person is crazy, or at least they think so). She added, "And whether you like it or not, whether you want to call him ex or whatever, he is still my husband! He always will be my husband, and you better get used to that! You don't know me! I will beat your ass until you scream for Black Jesus, White Jesus, Baby Jesus, Buddha and Mohammad for help!"

Still speaking calmly, I answered her, "You might try to beat my ass. You might even win, but you are going to know for many, MANY days that you were in a fight, bitch! I might look like you can beat my ass but looks can be very deceiving! Try me, hoe!"

I was ready! Boobs and all! I could see people walking on the parking lot, I was wondering if any of them were with her. But you know what, I didn't care!

"You don't want no part of me, bitch!" she warned me.

"YOU do not want any part of ME, bitch!" I raised my voice for the first time, I was standing solidly on my bare feet and I really didn't care. "And you know what? One of us may die on this parking lot tonight. Are you ready for that? Because right now, I really don't have a single, solitary DAMN to give about it!"

She clearly rethought. You can tell she was considering that I might be crazy too. She stepped back, noticing finally that my hand was in my purse. "Stay away from Kevin, bitch!" She walked away, and I watched her get in her car and head out the opposite end of the parking lot.

I saw Sean, one of the tenants in my building, and called to him. Just wanted someone to walk in with me. I didn't look for Kevin's car, and I didn't know whether to say something to him or not. Maybe he wasn't being an asshole; looks like she got a few extra servings of crazy before she left the womb.

It'd been nearly two months since the wedding. Greta and Cameron seemed very happy, and so did Gabby and Oliver. My job and I continue to have our ups and downs, but it also remains the most consistent tangible relationship in my life.

I have not seen Kevin Harper, Deputy Fire Chief AKA The light bulb man since I saw him at the firehouse and we haven't talked since I asked him to leave me alone. And I decided not to tell him about Michelle approaching me in the parking lot. If I approached him, I was certain I would have tremendous difficulty walking away. But I missed him. We lived in the same building, on the same floor, how can it be, that I never see him? It's probably for the best though. The *no longer lovely but crazy Michelle* would require some special handling, and I was not in the mood to make that kind of investment in her. I was still trying not to go viral!

To be honest, I'd cried my eyes out about this man. And as long as it'd been, I still cried from time to time when I thought about him. I don't think I really wanted him to stop talking to me. In fact, I know I didn't. I don't think I expected him to stop either.

I know that I was in love with him. But clearly, he was not in love with me. I had no choice but to be okay with that.

Alone again…naturally.

Chapter 18

Every Halloween, our building had a costume party. I had gone once or twice after living here for seven years. But I and the girls decided to go together this year. I needed to get out. Who knows, maybe I will see the light bulb guy again.

I had a lot of trouble deciding what to dress up as. We decided to all three dress up as *slutty nurses.* Of course, with Cameron as a patient and Oliver as a doctor escorting them, they couldn't be too slutty, especially when one was clearly pregnant!

It's actually a lot of fun so far though. Lots of people from the building and random others. A short guy, literally dressed as Napoleon, decided to troll me for the night. He thought I really was a slutty nurse! I started to think that I didn't want to be there anymore. And I really started to think about Kevin and how I almost had it good.

I became emotional but tried to hide it from my girls. I claimed a stomach-ache and let them know I was going home. I told them just stay and enjoy, but they said they will likely leave soon as well.

I was going to go—yes, binge *something yet to be determined* on Netflix and again yes—eat some black raspberry ice cream.

I hit the elevator button and turned my back to it, looking back at some of the guests still at the costume party. The gaiety of it all sort of saddened me even more.

The elevator bell rang.

I turned around to the open doors,

…and there…he was…

…standing there…on the elevator…

Superhero.

Fully costumed.

Superhero.

AKA *Kevin Harper, Deputy Fire Chief* AKA *the Light Bulb Man!*

He initially stood somewhat statuesque on the elevator, then stepped off saying, "Giselle, hi."

"Hi," I said. "It's good to see you."

"It's good to see you as well," he said. "How've you been?"

"I've been okay. Working hard," I said.

"Yes, I know. I see you from time to time," he said.

"But you've never said anything. You could have said hello!" I insisted.

"Well, you told me not to," he reminded me. "And things have kind of changed since I last saw you."

Of course, he's back with the *not lovely but crazy* Michele. I really didn't need this information!

"Oh," I asked, "how so?"

"I realised," he said, "that I don't like you so much."

"Gee, thanks!" Not such a great feeling was coming over me.

"I realised," he said, "that I really love you. I've thought of you every day since we've been apart. I seem to keep dwelling on what might have been. I love you so much and I've been trying to figure out how to get you back," he said. "I need you in my life."

"But you've never overtly acted on any of those feelings," I quietly reminded him.

"I know. I couldn't figure it out at first. But I came tonight, hoping to see you, to talk to you in some neutral place."

"Really?"

"Really."

"So why the superhero outfit though?" I asked. Remembering my dream from so many months ago.

"Because that's what I want to be for you. A man of steely devotion, who would turn the world in the opposite direction on its axis to save you from whatever. I want to rescue you, from whatever you, the strong woman that you are, cannot rescue yourself from. I want to be your *superhero,* Giselle. Will you let me do that? Will you let me be your superhero? Will you let me try, at least? Can you do that?"

"Yes," I said, nodding my head. "Yes. I can do that."

As I stood there in my superhero's arms, being kissed just like I wanted to be, I was reminded of Bridget. She used to say, "If we dare to dream, and we dare to believe, if we dare to put in the work—dreams do come true." Apparently, even when we do not realise that we are still hopeful for that elusive thing, it's out there somewhere looking for us. I would say just keep believing, keep being hopeful—because, looks like it really could happen!

CPSIA information can be obtained
at www.ICGtesting.com
Printed in the USA
LVHW051330040121
675400LV00006B/982